Private jets. Luxury cars. Exclusive five-star hotels. Designer outfits for every occasion and an entourage of staff to see to your every whim.

In this brand-new collection, ordinary women step into the world of the superrich and are

TAKEN BY THE MILLIONAIRE

Don't miss any of this month's offerings:

Dear Reader,

What is it that you love so much about Harlequin Presents Collections? Do particular themes have you on the edge of your seat? What does a sexy alpha male have to do to get your heart racing? You can share your views and find more information about books and authors at www.iheartpresents.com or you can e-mail us at presents@hmb.co.uk.

From next month, these collections will be known as Presents Extra. Be sure not to miss any of the titles in April 2008, when our heroines find themselves IN BED WITH THE BOSS!

Best wishes,

The Editors

HIRED FOR THE BOSS'S BED

ROBYN GRADY

TAKEN BY THE MILLIONAIRE

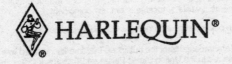

TORONTO • NEW YORK • LONDON
AMSTERDAM • PARIS • SYDNEY • HAMBURG
STOCKHOLM • ATHENS • TOKYO • MILAN • MADRID
PRAGUE • WARSAW • BUDAPEST • AUCKLAND

ISBN-13: 978-0-373-82074-0
ISBN-10:   0-373-82074-7

HIRED FOR THE BOSS'S BED

First North American Publication 2008.

Previously published in the U.K. under the title
DREAM JOB, HOT BOSS!

Copyright © 2007 by Robyn Grady.

This edition published by arrangement with Harlequin Books S.A.

® and TM are trademarks of the publisher. Trademarks indicated with
® are registered in the United States Patent and Trademark Office, the
Canadian Trade Marks Office and in other countries.

www.eHarlequin.com

Printed in U.S.A.

To my editor Kimberley Young for persisting, my agent Karen Solem for believing, and Rachel, Gail, Lisa and Mika for making the difference.

CHAPTER ONE

DON'T be such a baby. Feel the fear and, for God's sake, do it anyway.

Resolved, Serena Stevens gulped down a breath, raised a trembling fist and almost, *almost*, knocked on her boss's imposing double doors. But why the early summons before she'd even had time to hang her bag? Was it coincidence that today marked the end of her probation period?

Three months ago, David Miles, President of Miles Advertising Australia, had given Serena her first real break. At twenty-four, with a marketing degree but no experience, she'd been thrilled.

But was Mr Miles unhappy with her performance as Junior Account Executive? Would he roll back those impressive shoulders, furrow the steep slashes of his dark brows and level her with a stern, disapproving look? Did he want to discuss a demotion?

Her stomach back-flipped and her hand dropped like a weight.

Not a dismissal!

Beyond anything, Serena wanted to prove herself. Growing up with the nickname Miss Least-Likely-to-Succeed had not been pleasant. Chubby, self-conscious, a

delayed dyslexia diagnosis…school days were more for-
gettable than memorable. Thank God for her sense of
humour. Corrective tutoring, self-improvement books,
grooming courses and perseverance had eventually paid
off. Now the sky was her limit!

Sydney, with its big-city verve, café-culture and holiday
climate, would always be her true home. But as a teen
she'd felt so caged by her excess baggage and learning dis-
ability—add to that a father who questioned her every
decision—she'd vowed to some day break free and reach
every inch of her potential.

London, Paris, *New York*. Nothing and no one would hold
her back. Who knew when or even *if* she would ever return?

Serena pressed her lips together and kicked up her chin.

But first things first. She more than liked this job, she
needed it. 'Junior Account Exec' not only paid the bills, it
was an important step in her climb to the top.

After ironing damp palms down the sides of her white
jersey skirt, she crossed two fingers behind her back and
rapped on the timber. Before she could swallow the jet of
nerves clogging her throat, the right-side door swung open.
She smiled too hard and said the first stupid thing that
popped into her head.

'You rang?'

Mr Miles' deep blue eyes sharpened and one eyebrow
quirked before he gestured her in. 'Ms Stevens. Thanks for
coming so quickly.'

Tugging each onyx cufflink in turn, he accompanied her
to the guest chair adjacent his desk. Cheeks burning, Serena
slowly folded down as David Miles—top gun, millionaire,
hunk—sauntered around the bend of a long curved teak desk.

He ran a finger and thumb down an already perfectly

aligned crimson tie, which complemented a crisp white shirt. 'You must be wondering why I asked to see you?'

Did she see thunderclouds brewing behind those sooty lashes? Serena smothered a sigh. No use beating around the bush. If Mr Miles wanted to sack her, she might as well know now.

Heartbeat thudding in her ears, she watched him sit and draw in a high-backed chair. 'Is it bad?'

A muscle leapt in the square line of his jaw as he collected a pen and tipped it like a see-saw between middle finger and thumb. 'The news, Serena, is partly bad. But partly very good.'

She eased out a breath. Not fatal then. Her hand loosened its vice-like grip on the chair's armrest. 'As long as I'm not queuing for a new job next week, that's good enough for me.'

She couldn't be sure, but that twitch of his lip might have been a smile.

He sat back, his coal-black hair a little spiky, as if he'd shovelled a hand through it just before she'd arrived. 'You've heard we've won the *Hits* account?'

She perked up. 'The new music video programme? Sure. Everyone's saying it'll be the biggest thing to grace the tube since *Idol*.'

'You'd also know I hired Jezz McQade to plan and run the campaign.'

Yes, she knew, and had consequently read some industry pieces about this lady's vast achievements. 'Jezz McQade is the *best*. Any woman who can go from lead singer in an eighties rock band to a brilliant track record in advertising qualifies as a legend in my book. This year she's been working in the States, supervising top-name music-clips.'

Apparently pleased with her reply, he nodded, then laid both palms flat on the leather-bound day pad to push to his feet. 'As I said, there's some bad news. Jezz flew into the country from LA last night. This morning she slipped on some wet bathroom tiles.'

Serena cringed. Oh, God. 'Is she all right?'

'Broke her leg, the tibia, quite badly, I'm afraid. I received a call from Emergency. She hopes to be back on board—not without the help of painkillers and crutches—in seven, possibly eight weeks.'

How awful. But why tell her? Did Jezz McQade need a gofer?

Mr Miles crossed his arms over his broad deep chest and paced to where a run of silver award plaques, mounted on the far wall, shimmered in the artificial light. 'I have several senior people who might fill Jezz's shoes till she's back on her feet again. One in particular would climb over dead bodies to head this account.'

A name sprang to mind. 'Rachel Bragg.'

In large organizations, personality clashes and petty jealousies were bound to occur. A human relations manager on the ninth floor was employed to sort differences out. But Rachel…

Serena shuddered.

Suffice to say, *she* was a first-class witch. And Serena wasn't the only one who thought so.

Legs braced apart, David Miles concentrated on his words. 'Rachel is zealous about her position here. However, I'm more than aware of her shortfalls. She's an excellent account executive, but not the easiest person to handle.'

Excellent account executive? Oh, yeah. She'd heard *that* before. From Rachel.

David cocked his head and actually smiled. The expression touched his eyes and made them shine like prisms of blue light reflecting over water. 'You know, you really do have expressive features, Ms Stevens. Hope you don't play poker.'

She smiled. '"Expressive features." My high-school drama teacher used to say that. Can't count the number of times I had to demonstrate to my classmates elation, resentment, and, my absolute favourite, silly-buggers.' She pulled a face that included hooking her fingers in the sides of her mouth. When he laughed, she threw up her hands. 'Hey, at least I was good at *something*.'

An icy shaft fell through her middle.

Blabbermouth! Why stop there? Why not show him your junior-year photo, bottle-lense glasses and all?

But David Miles didn't bat an eye at her gaffe. Rather, he slid both hands into the pockets of his dark trousers, which had been tailored by a genius, and strolled over to the window. Eyes narrowed on the view, he picked up the thread of their previous conversation.

'After discussing it this morning, Jezz and I agreed the person we need should not only have knowledge of how things run around here, but also be able to bring a fresh look and natural enthusiasm to this product. Someone who has an affinity with pop culture, is in tune with demographics and has novel ideas on how to promote the show and its celebrities.' The ledge of his shoulders rotated back and he pinned her with a look. 'Someone like you.'

Serena's jaw unbolted and her mouth dropped wide open. She blinked several times at the shock, as well as a spike of doubtful excitement. 'You want…*me*?'

Soft lines branched from his eyes and the sweep of his

mouth relaxed as he moved forward to congratulate her.
'Yes, Serena. I want you.'

He cupped her hands to help her up. Trembling on
rubber-band legs, she sucked down a disbelieving breath.

'I don't know what to say. Except…' Emotion stung the
back of her nose as her shoulders thrust back. 'You won't
regret this, Mr Miles. I promise.'

Sandalwood, soap and masculine heat all registered as
those incredible eyes smiled down at her. 'David,' he said.
'It's time you called me David.'

Okay. Sure. She could do that. Just as soon as she got
her mind around this *wild* feeling. Nothing compared. Not
even accepting first place for her senior essay, 'Why and
How I Want to Succeed', in front of both her parents and
the entire school. That paper had been an effort to write.
But *this*! This was an unexpected gift from heaven.

Although five-foot-four could never compete with well-
over-six-foot, she drew up to her tallest.

'When would you like me to start?' Now? Yesterday?
'And you don't have to worry about my commitment, Mr
Miles. I'm totally yours, one hundred and ten per cent.
Weekends. Late nights. No sacrifice is too big.'

A pulse ticked in his shadowed jaw before he dropped
her hands and moved away. She gazed down and wiggled
her French-tips. Whoa. Her fingers were *tingling*.

'Serena, come over here. I'd like to show you something.'

She blinked up. Above a polished timber credenza desk,
which sat flush against the wall, that galaxy of industry
awards glittered out. David stood with his back to her, arms
folded, immaculate white oxford pulled tight between his
widely spaced shoulder blades.

Warmth seeped through her body.

Never mind those awards. *He* was impressive. His determination. That decadent chocolate-over-gravel voice. Best of all, his belief in her. *That* meant more than anything. Heck, if she were on the lookout for Mr Right, David Miles might well be the one.

She shook herself and moved to join him.

Good thing she wasn't. *Looking*, that was. Not now, not this year, not even this decade, or maybe the next. Career. Travel. Breaking free. Reaching the stars. Nothing and no one would hold her back. And this promotion meant she was truly on her way.

He nodded at a space on the wall. 'See that?'

By his side now—sandalwood, soap, *heat*—she tipped forward. Her contact lenses were in, however, 'I don't see a thing.'

'Exactly.' He dropped onto his haunches and yanked open one of four credenza doors.

As he rustled around inside, she enjoyed a bird's-eye view of those tailor-made trousers being tested over his squatting thighs—all rock-solid sinew was her guess, just like his arms.

After retrieving a gigantic spiralled notepad, he pushed up and thumbed through the pages.

His profile shot. Straight nose, Hollywood strong jaw, small scar interrupting the wing of his left brow...

Her gaze fluttered down.

And a prime-time chest. Very agreeable, in a way she'd never quite sensed about any guy before. Must be the 'older man' thing. Weren't they supposed to be sexier, smarter, somehow forbidden? Not that she should think about her boss that way. Even if she were looking. Which she was not.

He bent the book wings back over one another. 'This

diagram,' he said, 'summarizes the agency's history, clients and revenue. Here's where we began.' A long blunt-tipped finger slid up the paper in a forty-five-degree angle. 'This is where we are now.'

Head bowed, she scuffed a fall of fair hair behind an ear and held it back. At a glance, the red and yellow lines indicated a steady yet extraordinary performance in the marketplace. Except...

'What happened here?' She tapped an area near the start where the values spiralled to an alarming point, in fact, beyond the line of the X axis.

Her fingers barely escaped as he clapped the book shut. His words grated out. 'Bad judgment call. Hasn't happened since. Won't happen again.'

David slid the book away across the desktop, then turned to lift a hip and one of those muscular thighs over the credenza's edge. Loosely laced hands, big and tanned, fell between his parted legs as he locked her gaze with his.

'I'll be honest with you, Serena. I not only need this campaign to do well, I need it to do *exceptionally* well. I need the top prize at the Awards to fill that space. The international sponsors of *Hits* have assured me that if we take out gold for their account this year, we've got the rest of their business, an astronomical coup. If not...' His nostrils flared the barest amount. 'They'll take their business elsewhere and many others will follow. Miles Advertising's reputation—my reputation—will be manure.'

The enormity of it began to press in. *This* was the chance she'd waited for. Her springboard into an exciting future.

Her stomach muscles double-clutched.

But, given all the facts, this seemed almost *too* big. She'd faced challenges before, but this wasn't just about her. Her performance would affect others, most particularly the president of this company, her boss. What if she messed up? What if she couldn't deliver? What if her best wasn't enough?

Her hip met the credenza edge as blood rushed to her feet and her forehead prickled hot and cold. 'Is it okay to be terrified about now?'

He chuckled and the rumble comforted her, even if her smile was still wobbly.

'Nothing wrong with feeling fear. It's natural. Some might even say *necessary*.' His gaze intensified. 'As long as you can push through to the other side, learn to adapt, and do what needs to be done.'

Feel the fear, do it anyway. She nodded. Of course he was right.

He eased back. 'I'll be fully involved and Jezz is ready to hold it together from her sickbed, but…'

She finished the sentence. 'You're depending on me.'

His eyes dared hers. 'You ready?'

Ready as I'll ever be.

Keen to start, she set her mind to the task and stood up extra tall. Something crackled under her foot. Both his gaze and hers dropped. She bent first to retrieve…

'A paper plane?' She fired looks into every corner of the enormous office…at the granite and stainless steel wet bar, around the huge desk, then the black leather settee. 'You have a son tucked away in here somewhere?'

A bracket formed around one side of his mouth. 'Not here. Not *anywhere*.' She weighed the injured plane in her palm, then bogus-tested her throwing arm. 'It works better if you hold it further down toward the nose.'

She studied the plane, then the sophisticated man

perched on the desktop, one leg swinging. She must be mistaken. 'You're telling me this is *yours*?'

He reclaimed his property. 'Only if you're done with it.' His bottom lip jutted as he concentrated to smooth out the crumpled bits. 'After a couple of modifications to the cobra design, I was rather pleased with this one's performance. Exceptional gliding ability. Not sure about the landing.'

Collecting stocks, bonds, antiques, thoroughbreds…but *paper planes*?

A small laugh coughed out.

David's gaze kicked up and brows swooped together. 'What's so funny? It's not as if I wear ladies' underwear on weekends.' He examined the plane. 'This is a good, clean boys' pastime.'

'Exactly. It's a *boy's* pastime. And you're—' She bit her tongue. *Big Mouth Stevens strikes again.*

His head slanted and he set the plane down. 'You were going to say *old*?'

She lied. 'Of course not!'

With lazy grace, he slid off the credenza and turned around to stand before her. 'It's okay. I'm aware of the age difference. Thirty-two must seem ancient.'

Ancient? Or doable?

She stomped on that notion and averted her gaze to her fingertip doodling figure eights on the desktop. 'It's just that you seem so dedicated and nose-to-the-grindstone. I never pictured you…' the figure eights stretched longer '…never thought of you as…'

'Fun?' A crooked finger under her chin urged her to look up. 'At least not on the days I need my walking stick.'

She met his amused eyes as his knuckle grazed her jaw

line and fell away. Cue those tingles again, but this time they'd taken over her neck, stomach, *breasts*.

Her arms knotted over her chest. 'I didn't say that.'

'But you wanted to.'

'A walking stick never entered my mind.'

'Dentures, then?'

Damn. Now his eyes were laughing at her.

She dropped her arms. 'I only meant that I had this "all work and no play" concept of you.'

Which was pretty much the same concept she had of herself. She had a personal mountain to climb. Little time was left for recreation, a choice she had no problem with. None at all.

'Still, no one can spend *every* minute working,' she added. 'You have to break free some time or you'll fall over. Either that, or *explode*.'

A line formed between his brows, as if he'd never thought of it quite that way. As if it made perfect sense. As if…she'd somehow reached out and touched a well-hidden part of him.

A shiver raced over her skin.

More tingles? Had he moved closer? Suddenly those broad shoulders seemed even bigger.

She backed up, hit the desk and the bump set her off again. 'Everyone needs a release valve to ease the pressure. A hobby, like painting or yoga. I used to collect stamps.' Question marks formed in his eyes. She waved off his surprise. 'That's another story. Point is, now I think about it, making planes isn't *that* quirky.' His chin pulled in at 'quirky'. 'Anyway, you probably have *heaps* of other diversions.'

Uh, you can shut up now, Serena.

But she always rambled when she was nervous, and *he*

was making her more nervous than ever. Not saying a word. Just looking. And breathing. A little too deeply.

Oh. That was her.

His gaze turned curious as it dipped to skim her lips. 'You know, there is one other thing I love to do to relax.' A grin hooked his mouth and his eyes melded with hers again. 'Don't know that you'd call it a diversion.'

The distance between them definitely narrowed that time. She might have imagined it before, but just now he had taken a step towards her. Make that two.

'What—' She swallowed. 'What would you call it, then?'

His gaze licked the hollow of her throat. 'Well, it's nothing like collecting stamps.'

'Not stamps, huh?' Parched tinder sparked and crackled at her core. She tried to shrug. 'Cards? Tennis maybe?'

Nude Twister?

Which might be a whole lot closer. Was she imagining the answer glittering in his eyes? What was the bet his diversion started with S, and it wasn't singing in the shower?

As he crowded that bit more—*heat, lots and lots of heat*—her neck arched back and toes curled.

His absorbed gaze probed hers. 'Do you want to find out, Serena? Maybe do something you never dreamed of doing with me?'

Holy Moses! Had she got this right? Was he asking if she wanted him to press in close? Have him wind his arms around her, drop his head and kiss her till that delicious ache low in her belly became unbearable and she forgot her own name?

Sure, he was sexy; he didn't need to try. Intelligent and charming, too. But did she want to take that irreversible step and maybe get naked with her boss? This wasn't in her plans. Who knew he even fancied her?

'Is that a no?' His grin turned wicked. 'Or yes?'

Knees gone to water, she clutched the credenza's edge at each side, dredged up a *'Maybe?'* and felt both wanton and halfway okay with it.

His warm breath stirred her hair as his gaze roamed her face. 'I promise age won't affect my performance. In fact, experience makes all the difference here.'

Her drugged eyelids drifted shut, dragged open. Pulse rate soaring. Mind floating. *Everything* tingling. Was this really happening?

She groaned over a weak smile. 'Guess there's only one way to find out.'

He was almost upon her. *'Precisely.'*

She melted as one powerful arm reached out, and...

Kept going?

He muttered an apology and leaned around her. Something—a panel?—slid open behind her. He rocked away and presented a handful of...

She collapsed against the wood. 'Are those darts?' Heart in her throat, she spun around to the wall.

'And a dartboard.' He set about preening three sets of black and red feathers. 'I had that board built into the wall first week I leased this building. You made me realize I should bring it out more often.' He offered the darts. 'Wanna play?'

Geez, I really thought I did. But...

Lava sizzling through her system cooled as the ground once again turned solid beneath her feet. Feeling foolish, and determined to keep it to herself, she shook her head. 'Thanks, but I, um, think I should get back to my desk and clean my slate.'

'Sounds like a sensible idea.' He set the darts down next

to the plane, then ran a hand through his hair. 'I'll be in contact later today.'

When his palm hovered at the small of her back as he ushered her out, she stiffened rather than dissolved. Today the deficit between her largely celibate lifestyle and fantasy had played merry hell with her imagination. She shuddered to think of the scene had she puckered up when the last thing on David's mind had been foreplay. No doubt she'd have been demoted, in his mind and this office, to 'silly love-struck girl' rather than 'capable career-driven woman.' She'd make certain she didn't misunderstand him again.

They paused as he hauled open the door. Back in employee mode, where she belonged, she ended their meeting in an appropriate manner.

'Thank you for this opportunity, Mr Miles.' She went to shake his hand, but thought better of the physical contact.

'Call me David, remember?'

A ribbon of fresh excitement drew a smile across her face. 'I'm going to do such a fantastic job on this account, you'll never want to let me go.'

But, of course, Jezz McQade would be back on board soon enough. And what about those overseas plans? No forgetting her ultimate goal.

'Never let you go?' David's jaw shifted. 'Serena, I'm afraid you might be right.'

Did Mona Lisa have a brother? A dozen different emotions might be read into his expression…confidence, anticipation, lust.

Uh-oh. Time to go.

When the door closed, she passed Tilda, David's secretary, who wiggled friendly fingers, then pushed large round spectacles back up her nose. Serena returned the wave, humming. She'd discovered three, make that four, important things today.

One. At last someone valued her enough to truly take her seriously. After years of her protective dad obsessing over her every decision, this was a monumental step.

Two. She had zero interest in darts.

Three. Like it or not, David Miles and his shoulders turned her on.

Four. Now more than ever she couldn't afford to be distracted, definitely not by a relationship. Still it was clear she needed some form of relief—something brief but satisfying. She wasn't 'adventurous'; never had been. But, at this point in her life, could she possibly consider a one-night stand?

An absurd thought struck and the humming stopped.

Could David?

David crossed back to his desk and collected the paper plane, all the while thinking of Ms Stevens. Bright, amusing, sexy Ms Stevens.

His chest tightened.

Forget *sexy*. Forget what had happened just now when business talk had turned to flirting and, mind on his pants— and hers—he'd almost scooped that beautiful wide-eyed blonde into his arms. He needed to *focus*, and not on rogue urges, but his company's survival, which meant keeping his largest, most influential client happy.

He must win that top award for the *Hits* campaign or his reputation and a decade of gut-slogging work would be down the drain. He might as well shut up shop and move to Alaska. No way could he risk lowering his defences by fantasizing over an employee, doubly so after what Serena had let slip on signing her contract three months earlier.

Hard creasing the plane's folds, he moved towards a window view of his city, complete with her vibrant blue harbour dotted with multicoloured sails and churning ferries.

Sydney might be his base, a source of his energy, but when she got her chance Serena aimed to be on the first airbus to fame and fortune. Not that ambition was a *bad* thing. He admired anyone's desire to follow a dream. A big reason he found Serena so alluring was her drive. But she affected him in other ways, and therein lay the problem.

Should Serena somehow end up in his arms—in his bed—she was right: it could prove very difficult to let her go. But he didn't do love and, while it might disappoint naïve Serena to hear it, he no longer did sacrifice. Not as far as matters of the heart were concerned, anyway.

He'd mixed work with pleasure once before and it had cost him everything, including his pride. Now nothing, particularly sexual attraction, interfered with his judgment. A modicum of distance and two feet firmly planted on the ground always served him best.

After soaking in the seamless blue sky—the clean sunshine glinting off the massive Opera House shells—David sank into his chair and nodded.

As good as Ms Stevens looked and smelled and no doubt felt, she was not a candidate for his personal life. But with regard to today's business crisis, she might well be the answer to his prayers. Serena's ambition, that effervescent need to spread her wings and aim for the sky, was exactly the ingredient he needed…with one reservation.

Given her enthusiasm, she might insist on reaching *too* high, beyond what was reasonable. Then, regrettably, he'd have no choice…

He threw the plane at the window and turned back to his desk.

He'd have to cut her from the account.

CHAPTER TWO

Two whole days and *nothing*.

Dressed in yellow baby-doll pyjamas, full glass in hand, Serena slammed the fridge door, straightened her towel turban, then scuffed her bunny feet slippers back over her kitchen floor. Before indulging in a lavender-scented bath, she'd drafted a dozen ideas for the *Hits* campaign. Next on the agenda? Pasting a new affirmation on her personal blog.

Tough times don't last, tough women do.

Yesterday, David had said he'd contact her later regarding the promotion. Only he hadn't. Nor had he today, other than to cast a nod in her direction as they'd passed in the corridor at five-thirty this afternoon.

'Go home, Serena,' he'd told her, not unkindly, yet not super positive, either. 'No need for you to hang back.' Then he'd gone into snooty though, it must be said, attractive Rachel Bragg's office and shut the door.

Doubts pecking at her brain, Serena sipped her Chardonnay, sweetened by red soda, and descended into the cushions of her calico-covered couch.

Had the promotion been a fantasy? When did the fireworks begin? And she didn't mean the kind that had exploded with such sizzling effect when her imagination had run riot in Mr Miles'—er, David's office yesterday. When she'd been struck dumb enough to believe that her boss had designs on her. That he'd wanted to let go, and not paper planes.

Let go with her.

But he was so mature and worldly and polished and rich, and she was...

Serena sighed and sipped again.

Her father would have a field-day shaking his head over that one.

But she wouldn't sit back and stew over the promotion question for ever. She'd confront David about it first thing tomorrow.

Definitely by noon.

Her cell, parked next to her PC on the coffee-table, sang out and she picked up.

'Serena—' the masculine voice on the end of the line sounded uncommonly clear '—what are you doing for the rest of the evening?'

Her heartbeat stalled then slammed into overdrive.

David!

Now?

The black-cat-with-ticking-eyes clock above the kitchen sink said 7:00 p.m. But she *had* told him 'day or night', and after her horrible tryst with self-doubt, dear Lord, she meant it more than ever.

'What am I doing this evening?' She put her glass down next to an empty chocolate wrap. 'Nothing special. Why?'

'I'll explain when I get there.'

'Get where?'

'Your apartment. I got the address from your personnel file. I'm pulling up outside now.'

What?

She shot to her bunny feet and fell over herself to find a second-storey view.

Although the sun had set over Manly beach, tourists still snapped shots on the pine-lined boardwalk, while neighbourhood couples strolled with prams, and joggers wove through the pedestrian stream. Directly below, a late-model black Mercedes cruised into the kerb. Serena held her sinking stomach as David swung out the driver's side, cell pinned to his ear.

Peering up, he shielded his eyes from the streetlight radiating down through palm fronds bobbing in the Pacific Ocean breeze. 'That you?' He waved. 'Number twenty-four, yes?'

She couldn't answer. Could barely think. *This* was how a poor kangaroo stuck in headlights must feel…fixed to the spot, crippled by fear.

David swept around the back of his car. He was dressed all in black. She was dressed in…*kiddies-ville lingerie*.

'Serena? You there?'

Actually, no. She was flying into the bathroom, whipping the towel from her head, preparing for action. She'd been 'stuck in headlights', lacking the confidence to charge forward, too many times when she was younger. But she wasn't Miss Least-Likely-to-Succeed anymore. She was a professional, ready to take on the world!

Just as soon as she found her toothbrush.

Shoulder vice-gripping the cell to her ear, she spotted the pink handle hiding behind a bottle of body spray, which would one day be Chanel No 5.

'I'm here,' she replied, smearing paste on the brush.

'Sorry for the inconvenience.'

She kicked off the slippers. 'No inconvenience,' she managed around a mouthful of mint. 'See you in five.'

Near her front door, his deep voice echoed out through the building's security intercom. 'Make that two. Can you let me in?' She spat in the sink and dabbed her mouth dry. 'Serena?' Three beats of silence. 'Hello? Is there a problem?'

Out of the bathroom, she scooted by the intercom panel and punched a key. In her bedroom, she threw the cell onto the patchwork duvet, dived into her side drawer and yanked out the first set of underwear she could find…admittedly white cotton briefs were on top, but black silk was almost as handy.

Pyjamas off, panties and bra on.

The doorbell rang.

'Outfit, outfit…'

In her walk-in robe, pulse pounding in her ears, she shrugged into a mango-coloured wrap-dress with bell sleeves. Not exactly business diva standards, but, in a crisis, far easier to negotiate than a linen skirt suit. She swirled her almost-dry hair up into a twist. The doorbell rang again.

Power walking, she fixed her neckline, then put on the brakes, sucked in a breath and swung open the door.

There he stood, David Miles, incredibly up close and personal in a dark button-down that seemed to borrow from the shadow of his unshaven jaw. His gaze didn't waver from hers, yet the shivery sensation feathering up her spine, the glint in those knowing eyes, suggested he'd somehow taken her in from top to toe…every hair, every curve, every whirlwind thought.

Can he hear my heart thumping?

Congratulating herself on the composed smile, Serena waved him in. 'Come through.'

He offered a white grin at the same time she caught his scent, fresh and clean and hotter than ever.

'Not tonight.' He finger-combed what she guessed was shower-damp hair. 'We've got a lot to fit in.'

The vision of him soaped up under a warm spray, possibly singing, vanished. *A lot to fit in?* 'We do?'

'Slip some shoes on and we'll get going.'

Ready to fly to Mars and back, she retraced her steps to the bedroom and whipped on some white ballet flats. Almost to the doorway again, she slapped her forehead and wheeled back around. When she found the pendant, it tinkled against its small crystal bowl.

Jewellery wasn't her thing. One watch and a few pairs of earrings pretty much summed up her collection. But this gold heart and chain were beyond special. Only weeks before passing away, her mother had had a piece of her own necklace remodelled into this heart for her sixteenth birthday. Since then it had reminded her, not only of her mother, but also of Marion Stevens' belief in her only child, in Serena's decisions and her future. In eight years she hadn't forgotten it once, not even almost.

Until tonight.

After clasping the whisper-thin chain around her neck, she pressed the heart close to her own, then grabbed her carryall on her way past the hallstand and joined David in the outside corridor.

'This could be a late one.' His tucked-in chin and tone made it a question: *Still time to change your mind?*

As if.

Bursting to begin, she shut the locked door behind her. 'No sacrifice too big, remember?'

A muscle flinched in his cheek. 'Yeah. I remember.' He set off towards the lift, his stride longer than usual.

Belted up in the luxurious grey leather interior of his car a few moments later, Serena stole a look at David's profile as he flicked a glance at the rear-view mirror and pulled away. Then it dawned.

Opening her apartment door tonight, she'd been overwhelmed by the feeling that he'd somehow taken in every inch of her. They'd been standing close and his eyes had remained only on hers, yet he'd asked her to put on shoes before they left. It wasn't important. Still…

How had he known her feet were bare?

Bright red polish.

On autopilot, David stopped the car at a set of traffic lights and inwardly groaned.

First he'd been struck by those glistening ocean-green eyes, next, that healthy complexion, then her *toes*, for Pete's sake, wiggling away in his lower peripheral vision.

He tilted his head and blinked into space.

Could toes be classed as kissable? He'd never thought so before. What was the likelihood of developing a foot fetish this late in life? More importantly, what could be done about it? Cures, solutions, existed for every problem. Even attractive, increasingly tempting ones.

In the passenger seat beside him, Serena shifted and crossed long silky-smooth legs. Thank God she wasn't wearing sandals; that sight was dangerous enough as it was.

'Mind if I ask where we're going?' she asked.

He took her in, so alert and unwittingly seductive, and his brain fogged up and nether regions squeezed tight. Just like yesterday in his office when a harmless tease had got out of hand. For one heated moment he'd thought she might have gleaned his less- than-innocent meaning. But when he came to his senses and remembered the dartboard, he was sure she had dismissed any improper ideas.

No harm, no foul.

Accelerating now the lights were green, he exercised his neck and tried to focus.

Distance...a modicum of distance...

'We're seeing Jezz McQade in hospital,' he told her. 'They okayed her for visitors an hour ago.'

'Isn't it kind of late?'

He frowned. 'Jezz is as eager to get this ball rolling as I am.' *As I thought you were.*

'I only meant that visiting hours usually finish at eight, don't they?'

'That still gives us—' the luminous dash clock said 7:07 '—maybe thirty minutes. We've lost enough time.'

'You can say that again.'

Had he heard that soft scoff and mumble right? 'I beg your pardon?'

'Oh, nothing, nothing.'

His gaze left the multi-lane road. If he could make out her expression he'd have some clue, but in the shifting shadows of the car cabin he could only be sure she was chewing her lip. That closest dimple working double time in her cheek upped her sex-appeal factor by roughly one thousand per cent.

His fly flexed and he groaned again.

This can't go on or I'll be walking on three legs by the end of the night.

'For heaven's sake, Serena, *speak up.*'

Though she tried to hide it, he felt her shrink into her seat.

Terrific. Ten negative points to the jerk in the front row. She was young, inexperienced. The last thing he wanted was to crush her. Still, this wasn't a drill. As much as she needed to be able to gauge when silence was golden, equally she should learn when to share, particularly with him. Had he been wrong about her ability and drive? Did she have the wherewithal to even see this through?

Where were those kid gloves?

'We're playing with big chips,' he said as a bus full of swaying commuters hurtled past. 'And if this is going to work, we need to keep the communication lines wide open. In our situation, there's no room for insecurity or second-guessing each other.'

'I know,' she murmured. 'I only meant…well, I'd begun to think I might have dreamt it all.'

The car peaked over a crescent and a twinkling sea of city and bridge lights swam into view. 'Dreamt what? The promotion?' Remembering her exuberant reaction, he smiled. 'That was no dream.'

'Actually, I thought maybe you'd changed your mind.'

He corrected the wheel after he cut her a glance and the car jerked left. 'You thought *what*?'

Uncrossing her legs, she rubbed anxious palms up and down the silky fabric resting on her thighs. Nice thighs, he'd wager. Probably even nicer than those calves. Those toes…

Argh. Distance, damn it!

'When you didn't call,' she said, 'I thought you might have changed your mind. The only time you saw me, you…'

Imagining her lips pressed together, he lowered his brow. 'Communication lines, Serena, remember?'

She sighed, then rushed it out. 'You ignored me.'

He barked out a laugh. 'I didn't *ignore* you. I simply told you not to hang around—' He paused.

Which did sound rather ambiguous, come to think of it.

But he'd fix that now. Lead by example. No mix-ups or mixed messages, calm and clear, then everyone knew where they stood and no one's expectations could be let down. Not hers and definitely not his.

'Forget I spoke.' She chewed a nail. 'I shouldn't have said anything.'

His eyes cut back to the road. 'The last thing I want, the very last thing we need, are misunderstandings.'

Out the corner of his eye, he saw her hand leave her mouth. 'I agree.'

'I should have caught up with you sooner. But I meant what I said. I'm relying on you to help pull us through this sticky patch. Nothing's changed since yesterday.' This situation *would* work—it had to. A thought from left field struck. 'Did you bring a notepad?'

'I always carry one.'

He indicated and took an inner-city street not far from the hospital. 'Well, then, hang onto your hat, because...' *for better or worse* '...this ride's about to begin.'

CHAPTER THREE

SERENA enjoyed the delicious shiver that tripped up her spine, not only at David's words, but also his bone-melting smile.

In hindsight it had been ridiculous to think that a professional like David would drop her with no good reason. He wasn't the sort to make snap decisions, and she was resilient, motivated, tenacious, proving herself more with every step, even tiny ones. When would she stop beating up on herself?

She gazed out the window as a stream of boutique fronts, displaying summer fashion, flickered by.

Growing up, how she'd envied girls who didn't worry about wearing bikinis, or sitting exams, or talking to boys…*kissing* boys, sometimes going further. Whenever the lights went down at parties, instead of cuddling up, she would always sneak out. No matter how she tried to overcome it, to even think of kissing made her blush all over.

The next day her girlfriends would swap stories and dream about their future Prince Charmings—what he'd looked like, where he'd live, what he'd be. Serena had never had a clear picture, but as David swung the car into the hospital entrance and parked, an accurate image formed in her mind.

He'd be dark-haired, commanding, serious but with a

dash of rogue. A man who would support her decisions, but never stifle her. Who took from her what he wanted, and made her helpless but to want it all the time.

All that was such a long way off. Still...

Breaking off her sidelong glance at his profile, Serena smiled.

She could dream, couldn't she?

When they entered a hospital lift, David struck a button and stepped back, holding his clasped hands in front.

'More than anything, this will be a getting-to-know-you meeting,' he said. 'We'll discuss some of the ideas Jezz might have on the campaign's direction since we last spoke. Then she and I need to sort out a few logistics.'

'Sounds good.' Mind back on work, she followed when David strode out between parting metallic doors. 'I'll take lots of notes.'

He stopped and let her catch up. 'Did you remember to bring a pencil to go with that book?'

When his lips twitched, she relaxed. 'Several, thank you very much.'

They fell into step before he asked more seriously, 'You take shorthand?'

Her stomach flipped and tongue grew thick in the mouth as she fibbed. Longhand had been difficult to master. 'Not very recently.'

They passed a gallery of outback landscape prints and followed the signs to the ward. 'You learnt it at school then?' he asked. 'Or were you into all the creative subjects, like your drama class?'

'I left my drama days behind in my mid-teens. In university I took business subjects, but not shorthand.'

'I doubt it's too popular any more.'

Two nurses padded by in their white soft-soled shoes as Serena thought about it. 'Guess it was different in your day.'

'Oh, in my day,' he said, 'pigeons were the preferred mode of sending and receiving messages. Those stone tablets were just too darn heavy to lug to the post office.'

She laughed, then realized her insult. 'Sorry, I only meant—'

A grin captured the corner of his mouth as he stopped and planted his feet to peer down at her. 'Want some simple advice?'

She shrugged. 'Absolutely.' Anything and everything he had to offer.

'Unless there's something to apologize for, don't say sorry.'

His gaze brushed her face—the line of her cheek— before he set off walking again. A flurry of sensations danced over the fine hairs on her arms before she shook herself and followed.

'It can become a habit,' he was saying. 'People grow to expect it. Next thing you know you've apologized for something that you're not responsible for. And, believe me, there's enough genuine obligation to go around without taking on unnecessary weight.'

His advice sounded almost mercenary, yet obvious. Her smile was wry. 'Is that what *you* learnt at school?'

'No. From life.'

His blunt reply hit her in the solar plexus. She knew so little about him—his background, childhood, what experiences had moulded the man he'd become. What made him laugh or angry or sad. 'Sounds as if you've had some tough lessons.'

His furrowed gaze slid over to her. She almost let slip an apology for prying, but stifled it.

He nodded, apparently pleased by her stand, then tipped his chin as they approached a closed door. 'That is Jezz's room.'

They reached the doorway, but he didn't knock. Instead, standing close, his shirt inches from her shoulder, she sensed his gaze burning down. Heart beating fast, she tilted her face up to his. His eyes held hers for a long penetrating moment before he spoke.

'Some people appear to have charmed lives, Serena. Others can't seem to cut a break. Whether you're from the first batch, second, or a combination of the two, one of the toughest yet most important lessons is, know yourself well enough to never make the same mistake twice, because life is full enough as it is. Full of challenges and choices, decisions and disappointments, wishes lost—' his voice deepened '—and passions found.'

Her every atom flashed hot as the air was sucked clean from her lungs.

He was talking as her boss, right? Logic told her so, yet his eyes searching hers set her blood on a slow boil. A pulse leapt down a cord at the side of his tanned neck as his gaze seemed to distance yet, at the same time, *caress* her. It left her light-headed…out of breath…quivering…

He straightened, rolled his broad shoulders back and the spell was broken. 'Let's meet Ms McQade, shall we?'

He knocked, then vanished through the opened door. She stared at the space he'd occupied as an avalanche of emotion plunged through her.

What was that about not making the same mistake twice?

But it wasn't imagination this time. She *had* seen a gleam of desire in the depths of his eyes. Felt flames from his body lick out to singe hers. Incredible, but if she was right and this attraction was real, where did they go from here? What did it mean? No end of complications, problems, pitfalls?

She drifted through the doorway.

Or a chance to let go, just once?

Inside the private hospital room, Serena was snapped from her daze by a vision of vibrant red hair splayed over an enormous boomerang pillow.

'Hope you guys brought a marker.' Propped up on a hydraulic bed, Jezz McQade indicated her plastered leg. 'Rules are, no autograph, no visit.'

The friendly smoke'n'whiskey voice was a perfect partner for the informal air. Serena could easily picture Jezz, somewhere in her late forties, in a pair of flares, belting out some earthy rock ballad on stage, giving the audience every ounce of grunt she owned.

Chuckling, David moved forward. Serena pushed away the remnants of the episode outside and followed.

David found Jezz's hand and pumped it once. 'Good to finally meet you. This is Serena Stevens, the account executive I spoke with you about yesterday.'

Serena's heart grew when Jezz's face lit up with interest. She accepted the hand David had released. 'Glad to meet you, Ms McQade.'

Jezz brought her other hand over to cement the handshake. 'Ditto. But there's one thing we'll get straight from the start. No *Ms McQade*.' The momentary growl was replaced with a smile. 'Call me Jezz.'

Serena relaxed more. 'Jezz it is.'

Outfitted in a black and orange Snoopy nightshirt, Jezz gestured to a couple of nearby chairs.

'I'm known to be clumsy,' she said, reaching for a flat

white box on the bedside table as they took a seat. 'But this takes the klutz cake of all time. Big tip, hon,' she said to Serena. 'Never listen to your favourite dance number in a steamy bathroom, even a beautiful big marble one.' She skipped her attention to David as she tugged and the box's blue ribbon unravelled. 'Gorgeous accommodation, thank you, David. Hopefully I'll get back to that view soon. But first things first.' She whipped off the lid and offered a selection of milk chocolates. 'I recommend the almond centre.'

David waved a polite hand, but Serena accepted. Seemed she and Jezz would get along just fine.

Jezz selected a Turkish delight. 'We're short on time—' she popped the chocolate '—so let's get this party started.'

David reached into his trouser pocket and retrieved a mini voice-activated recorder. He sent Serena a wink. 'I always like a backup.'

Jezz took on a professional persona as she and David fell into an intense conversation incorporating various aspects of the campaign's development. Artwork, photo shoots, scripts, co-ordinating print, radio and television with talent. Phew! Incredibly interesting but a little out of Serena's depth. All the more reason for stacks of notes.

She gave the recorder a run for its money and was blowing on worn fingers when the conversation turned to strategies concerning the campaign's basic component, the younger generation and their music.

Finished downing water from a tall glass, Jezz smacked her lips. 'So, how would you like to follow up on some artists appearing on the debut show? Make inquiries into lead-in interviews and related advertising?'

Serena choked up. Jezz had spoken to *her*? About

artist interviews? This was it! The first assignment of real responsibility.

She couldn't help grinning from ear to ear. 'I'd love to.' So aware of David and his encouraging gaze, Serena hitched forward, ready for the details.

But a wiry-looking nurse burst into the room to announce in a crisp tone, 'Medication time!'

Groaning, Jezz fell back against the pillow. 'That must be the first line you gals learn at nurse school.'

The nurse pursed her rouged mouth and responded in a bone-dry tone, 'Thank your stars it's not a suppository.'

David jumped from his seat as though its chequered padding had caught fire. 'We've held you up long enough.'

Serena got to her feet too, but Jezz raised a hand. 'Do me a favour?' she said to David. 'Grab a cola from the vending machine down the hall. Serena'll catch up in a tick.'

David sent a supportive smile. 'Sounds like a plan.' With long easy strides, he crossed to the door. 'I'll wait outside.'

Jezz patted the pale blue crocheted spread. 'This is a big break for you, isn't it, hon?'

Serena eased herself down on the bed and nodded.

Jezz's eyes were the colour of a full glass of beer held up to the light. They half-mooned now above an understanding smile. 'Feeling all excited and jittery at the same time?'

'It's the worst feeling.' Serena visibly shuddered then grinned. 'And the *best*.'

Jezz gazed off at some imaginary spot as the nurse clipped a blood-pressure gadget to her middle finger. 'I remember when I was your age. I wanted to take the world by storm.'

Serena laughed. 'And you *did*.'

'My band days were the best. Didn't need but a couple

of hours sleep. We'd jam all night and travel all day. Everything was so new.' She chuckled. 'And just a little overwhelming for a country girl.'

Serena set aside the notebook, crooked up a leg and slotted the ankle under her other knee. 'I thought your hometown was Sydney.'

'Not originally. I hail from a little farming town in Queensland. Lived there till I was sixteen. Then something just clicked inside of me and I knew things were about to change.'

Serena nodded. 'I know exactly what you mean.'

It was like an alarm clock ringing deep inside, a feeling that couldn't be switched off.

Jezz pushed out a breath. 'I couldn't *wait* to get out of that one-road town and see everything the world had to offer.' Her nose and its bump scrunched as she inclined her head and smiled. 'Hear what I'm saying?'

Loud and clear. She'd come a long way since the days when homesickness and insecurities had stopped her from going to school camp or even staying a whole weekend at a friend's place. Her parents had been great about it, encouraging but never pushing too hard. Her dad had been different back then.

'I love Sydney,' Serena said, 'but I'm dying to live overseas.' Her face went hot. *Oh, God, foot in mouth again.* She sat up straight and tried to shrug it off. 'That's some time in the future, of course. Not any time very soon.' *I am so here for you and David and this campaign.*

But Jezz was caught up in memories. 'Travelling's a fantastic experience. Sydney's no backwoods, but Britain, the States, Europe. Every woman deserves to do Paris at least once, if not for the fashion, then the pastries.' Her smile changed. 'Ten years ago, no one could've told me how good it'd feel to get back home.'

Serena rationalised that statement. 'You must be looking forward to seeing your family.'

'Both my folks are gone now.'

Jezz's eyes shone with a regret Serena identified with. Age knew no boundaries as far as the pain of losing someone you love was concerned. 'I'm sorry.' She meant it to her very soul.

'I have a kid brother though. He has two girls. Or they *were* girls. Must be women in their early twenties by now.' The nurse with the lips rattled chart pages at the end of the bed while Jezz blinked several times. 'Makes me wonder how my life might have turned out if I'd met the right one.'

'You never fell in love?' Too personal a question? Perhaps. But Serena guessed her new mentor didn't mind in the least.

Jezz waggled thin copper-coloured eyebrows. 'Fell in lust a few times. Don't know that it was love. Another chocolate?' She reached for the box, but Serena shook her head. She'd hate herself enough tomorrow. 'What about you? Cupid ever shoot you with an arrow?'

Me? In love?

Serena's mind went blank, probably because there wasn't a whole lot to tell, even after high school. Then a vision of the dark-haired man, commanding, serious but with a dash of rogue, came to mind. Was it lust—?

'Visiting hours finish in five, ladies.' The nurse slipped the pen behind an ear and disappeared out the room.

'Better get back to business.' Jezz ruffled the tissue paper over the two remaining soft centres and edged the box aside. 'You'll do great,' she told Serena. 'Each day I'll lay out the groundwork. We'll communicate through phone, email and in the evening we'll have an update meeting—'

A double rap on the door and David poked his head in. 'Hate to bust up the party, but it's almost eight and we still have work to do.'

Jezz shot glances between the two. 'You're going back to the office *now*?'

'Not the office. But we have a short walk ahead of us, so—' David flipped a beckoning hand at Serena '—grab your bag. We'll leave Jezz to rest.'

A ripple of anticipation stirred in her stomach as Serena joined him. Where did he plan to take her? Would other people be involved? Or would it be quiet and deserted but for them? And, if she were honest, which would she prefer? Strictly business? Or just him, her and a dozen possibilities?

As they walked together to the lift he went over their discussion with Jezz, but Serena couldn't help thinking how much her perception of David had changed from Monday morning to Tuesday night. In subtle ways…she hadn't realized his hair was long enough to lick the collar of his shirt. In disruptive but exciting ways, too…he might be her boss, but he was also a flesh and blood, sexual being.

Stupid to consider, detrimental to her position, her career, her *dreams*. Still, no getting around the fact. Every time she saw him, every time he smiled or talked or touched, he grew more attractive, more real life, more…

Irresistible?

CHAPTER FOUR

'WANT to know what I can't resist?' David filled his lungs as they continued their walk from the hospital down through harbour-side Circular Quay.

'What you can't resist?' Serena gave him an almost sheepish look. 'Um…why don't you tell me?'

Despite his vow to abstain from any illicit thoughts regarding his protégé, he could very easily have said, 'You.' Serena's enthusiasm, her *toes*, her innocent—or were they temptress?—eyes when she gazed up into his, drinking in his every word.

Forcing himself to concentrate on the ferry crowds streaming both ways from the harbour platforms, he sucked in another lungful of briny air. 'I can't resist this town at night.'

The energy, the beauty, the *sparkle*. It reminded him of Serena. Then again, lately everything reminded him of her.

When she didn't answer, he swung over a look. Her dimples were nowhere to be seen.

Unimpressed?

A pang curled in the pit of his stomach.

Of course. Her ultimate sights were set on distant lands, broadening her horizons, just like another woman he'd once known. It had taken years to rebuild his agency's client base, as well as his reputation, when Olivia Roundtree had flicked back her long dark hair and waltzed out on him *and* her position. No matter how desirable he found Serena, surely that life experience gave him enough reason in itself to stay clear. Enough reason to pretend this temptation didn't exist.

She pointed out an indigenous street performer, moving to the recorded drone of a didgeridoo. 'There's certainly plenty to see.'

'Funny. I'd pick you more for nightclubs over corroborees.'

From the look on her face, she'd spotted the tongue in his cheek. She wrapped her arms around her waist. The breeze was cool; he should have thought to bring the jacket from his car to offer her.

'I don't visit that scene much any more.'

'Too old?' he ribbed.

'Too busy,' she parried. 'What about you?'

He cast a glance over a shoulder at the Opera House. 'Clubs aren't my scene either.'

'More into Shakespeare and arias?'

He smirked. 'Just not into gyrating to deafening music.'

'Well, it's a darn good thing you've got me to help with *Hits*, then.' She buffed a set of nails on her upper sleeve.

'A fan of loud music, okay.' He'd play along. 'But how are you placed for gyrating?'

He enjoyed the flash in her eyes, the way she hugged herself more tightly, how her breasts pushed up and she didn't shy from his gaze.

'I must confess,' she said, 'I haven't done much lately.'

'Maybe we should fix that.'

She blinked before her gaze skated away, back to the scenery.

He shoved his hands deep into his pockets. Given their conversation's subtext, his self-analysis—this hard-on—he was headed for trouble. And, from her expression, he had to consider that she might be inviting it.

When she'd listened to his speech in the hospital doorway about wishes and passions, he'd thought he'd revealed himself. The best part of him hadn't wanted to. The more primitive part, however, kept right on pushing. After years of being content with inconsequential affairs, what was it about Serena Stevens that made her so darn special?

Deep in thought, Serena unravelled her arms and chuckled to herself.

His smile was reflex. 'What's so funny?'

'Our talk of clubs reminded me of a night out with the girls a couple of years back. Kirsty Dunn's twenty-first birthday. We'd done the family restaurant thing, then Kirsty wanted to paint the town red. We ended up at a party bar in Kings Cross.'

Australia's best-known 'hotspot'? This ought to be good.

'Kirsty had one too many Fluffy Ducks,' Serena said. 'She kept asking for Duffy—' She bit her lip. 'Well, you can fill in the blank. Anyway, Sally Freeman got it into her head to get a waiter, dressed as a cowboy, to perform a table dance. But Sally wasn't wearing her contacts and pointed me out instead. He came right over and asked me to tug on his chaps.'

She chuckled again, then sighed, a long, contented sound.

David waited, frown deepening. 'And? What happened next?'

She stopped, faced him and tacked her gaze to his. 'Only if you tell me first.'

His thinking faltered. What was she on about? He was damn sure *he'd* never pulled any guy's chaps.

She twisted her mouth and persisted. 'You're not going to tell me, are you?'

Did she want to hear about his own escapades? If he'd ever dressed up as a cowboy? Not recently, but if she was interested…

A hot band tightened around his chest and the air in his lungs burned up.

Was she interested? And if this attraction was mutual, if he'd read her signs right, should he be crazy enough to consider it? Should he break an iron-clad rule and taste forbidden fruit?

But if he experienced her just the once, held her close enough to breathe in her perfume and melt into her curves, perhaps he could get this craving out of his system. His hunger would be satisfied and it would be back to regular viewing. It wasn't as if she didn't have her own star to follow, and they were both over eighteen. Surely one night together wouldn't break her heart *or* his.

Serena rolled her eyes and groaned. 'What do I have to do? *Beg?*'

He clamped down on a muscle ticking in jaw.

He was done wondering.

'Beg?' He stopped to face her square on. 'Sure, if you like.'

'All right.' She clasped her hands under her chin in a prayer pose. '*Ple-e-ease.*'

As his gaze zeroed in on her lips a far-off merchant ship blew its horn. Long. Hard. His arms and legs grew strangely heavy. The ache in his gut, in his groin, overwhelmed every other sensation. As a rush of heat scored his flesh, his mind went blank, then flashed bright with neon colour.

Next he knew, his hands were cupping the slippery fabric sloped over her shoulders. He urged her in and his mouth searched out the treasure of hers. When she opened up, he found it, savoured it, and what was more, he couldn't get enough of it.

His hands trailed up to capture her warm face, to manoeuvre and work the kiss. Breathing deeply, pulse rate off the chart, he gave himself over to this one moment where he was nothing more than a man, defying the rules, denying everything but primal instinct. She felt *so* good.

A moan deep in her throat vibrated up to his lips, over his tongue. Her fingertips walked higher, pressed in, then kneaded his chest. How he wanted to return the favour.

Later. Yes, later.

Nowhere near ready, he forced himself to gently break away. The lively noise of the Quay, strangers milling and smiling as they cut around them, faded back into focus. Had he been aware of his actions? Was he bewitched or out of his mind? Not in the slightest. God help him, he wanted more.

Fighting the impulse to nuzzle into the flush of her cheek, he gazed into those pretty eyes, which flickered open now.

Mouth slightly parted, she focused, then found a soft, throaty voice. 'I want…'

A white-hot quiver sizzled through him. Oh, yeah, he wanted it, too. As soon as possible.

'Hmm? Tell me,' he murmured, nudging his pelvis closer, hands sliding down over her collar-bones to wing in her arms just above the elbow.

The slender column of her throat bobbed. She shrugged one shoulder. 'I just wanted to know where we were going.'

His heartbeat stalled as the full circle of his surroundings receded back till there was only Serena and him and this un-expected, awkward situation. He must have heard wrong.

'Where we're *going*?'

When she slowly nodded, his stomach dipped and he slid one long step back. Reality continued crashing in as he ground a hand back through his hair and remembered.

Work. The appointment they were now most certainly late for. The campaign his reputation depended on. The gold award that ensured not only his agency's continued success, but its survival.

He went to straighten his tie, remembered he wasn't wearing one and tugged an ear instead as they began to walk again.

Even up until an hour ago he'd fooled himself that he controlled this attraction, that he could quarantine and conquer it, as he did any weakness. His father had taught his eldest son the benefits of mind over emotion, a formula the wily barrister had applied to amass a family fortune. After a bad start, David had followed it religiously, until now, when he'd let an amusing interest develop into an overnight, king-sized tug-of-war. Impulse against common sense. Work responsibilities versus sexual need. But how did Serena feel?

You could bet he'd find out. Pretending this never happened wasn't the answer. They needed to talk. Unfortunately, that conversation would have to wait.

Two at a time, he took the steps to the well-known address while Serena followed dutifully behind. Breezing through into the building's black granite entrance, he answered her question. 'Actually, we're here. I organized for a sound studio to keep their doors open so we could listen to the score for *Hits*.'

'Really?'

He glanced over. Tell-tale warmth flooded his limbs at the sight of her sparkling sea-green eyes. 'Thought you'd be pleased.'

In an attempt to redeem himself over this afternoon's misunderstanding regarding her promotion, he'd kept this treat up his sleeve. He'd anticipated exactly her Christmas-light expression. Perhaps he should have been up front, as he would have been with any other employee. But then they'd have missed that stimulating conversation and the kiss of the century.

His fingers clenched, then flexed. 'You're probably aware this is considered the best recording studio in the country.' *Work, for now focus on work.* If she was mature enough to put their embrace behind them for the moment, surely so could he. 'Their reputation is unsurpassed here, as well as overseas. I know they'll have done a great job.'

'Are lyrics in the pipeline?'

David grinned. The lady was good. Soon they'd be listening to lyrics already incorporated into some of the mixes. But how quickly and confidently could Serena articulate her thoughts? She might turn his private dials up to overload, but foremost she had a job to do and she must do it well. That was paramount.

He tested her. 'Do you think we need words?'

She didn't hesitate. 'Absolutely. A piece of music might sprinkle goose-bumps up your legs, but lyrics speak to everyone uniquely. It's the words of a song that link you for ever with a moment in your life. You relive that emotion every time you hear it. Happy. Bummed out. Falling in love.'

She'd looked back over her shoulder at something. He couldn't see her face. Was she deliberately avoiding his gaze?

His forehead prickled.

And who said anything about *falling in love*?

In silence they rode the lift to the tenth floor, her face unreadable for the first infuriating time ever. He stretched his neck and grimaced. His collar felt tight and it wasn't even buttoned.

What was she thinking? Was that last comment a tease? Or innocent? That would explain her no-cracks expression. And she was right. After tonight, whenever he heard this score, he'd go back to when he'd held her face, the world had melted away and he'd shot to the stars enjoying their first kiss.

Their first but, hopefully, not their last.

The doors opened and they crossed the foyer's polished parquet flooring.

She nibbled her bottom lip, obviously mulling something over. 'Has anyone considered a run of instrumentals to high-light different musical styles? The composition should sound familiar to the public, but not generic or boring.'

Okay. Now he was impressed. Approaching the front desk, he nodded. 'Good point. Bring it up at the next meeting.'

A butter-wouldn't-melt-in-her-mouth smile set his blood alight. 'Your wish is my command.'

Oh, she could be his genie in a bottle any day.

'David Miles. Hello, mate!'

Inside the reception lounge, decorated with blinding metal cut-outs and rainbow shades of blue, David swung towards an English accent that belonged to Jonathon Sturts, Mixem Studios' hotshot company director.

Jonathon snatched a puzzled glance at his Rolex. 'What are you doing here this time of night? I was on my way to dinner. Did we have an appointment?'

David gave his hand in greeting. 'I'm booked in to catch a preview of the *Hits* track.' Chest expanding, he stepped aside to introduce the not only beautiful but also incredibly bright young woman standing behind him. 'Jonathon Sturts, meet Serena Stevens.'

Jonathon channelled fascinated fingers through his sweep of overly long fair hair. A slow, appreciative smile broke a heartbeat later. 'Pleasure to meet you, Serena.'

Serena stepped forward to accept the hand offered. 'Jonathon.'

'Unfortunately I'm already late for supper.' Grudgingly Jonathon returned his attention to David. 'I'd thought everything was put to bed, but I'll check on your booth.' With undisguised curiosity, he fixed upon Serena again. 'How would that do, my dear?'

Serena's white smile fanned wider. 'Sounds great.'

David's gaze shot between the two—Serena, then Jonathon, whose leer remained in the vicinity of her lips. Everyone knew this man's reputation: a maestro with music, a wolf with women. Normally it didn't matter a fig to David. But Serena was off limits. His mother had said her eldest had never learned to share and she was right.

Jonathon snapped curt fingers at a woman who was dressed in gothic garb and passing by in a hurry.

'Marissa?' Jonathon called her over. 'Do you know anything about David Miles' booking time this evening?'

The silver stud under his junior assistant's lower lip flashed beneath the lights. 'Nuh-uh. Must be a mistake. Everyone had to be out for the annual debugging. The pest-control guy's cancelled till next week, but I only found that out at six when people had already gone home. Which is where I'm headed...' she trailed off.

David stepped in. Making progress was a priority, but if their situation here couldn't be fixed, this night held other possibilities. 'No problem. We'll arrange another time and get out of your hair.'

'*Nonsense*,' Jonathon said and Marissa groaned. 'Marissa, open booth D for Mr Miles.' She swallowed an argument, then, shoulders slumped, dragged her army boots through a swinging door. Jonathon quirked a brow. 'Good help is so difficult to find.'

Serena's attention had wandered to a gallery of framed special edition posters lining the far wall.

Jonathon's aristocratic chin rose with an important air. 'We have a few notable contacts abroad.' He nodded at the posters, urging her on. 'Be my guest. It's an impressive line-up.'

David's irritation over their host's leering subsided. 'Appreciate you helping us out.'

Jonathon flicked it off. 'Don't mention it.'

'Frankly, it's been a madhouse at the agency lately. My plans seem shot to hell before the day even begins.'

'Never enough time in this business, either. My man in Piccadilly isn't helping any. I'd sack the sod in a blink if I could find a half-decent replacement.' Jonathon wound his arms over his chest. 'Suppose your lot's gearing up for the big awards. Not far off, eh?'

'A few months.' David's gaze remained on Serena, her innocent enthusiasm, her not-so-innocent curves.

'This account should offer some first-rate fodder for the committee to chew on?'

David nodded. 'That's the plan.'

For years, his world had revolved around his agency's ascent. After that God-awful start with Olivia, slow and steady had paid off. He was almost there. Then everything he'd busted his royal butt over would be truly acknowledged. He could rest easy knowing that he'd made the best of a vocation that had very much been a second choice.

That couldn't be helped. Choosing to be there for his family when his father was ill instead of joining the air force had been tough. Hell, he'd wanted to be a pilot since before he could remember. But it hadn't been a sacrifice so much as simply the right decision. Just as it was the right decision now to place his career before anything else.

An eye on Serena, David chewed his inside cheek.

Jonathon's attention slid back to Serena, too. His almost feline eyes gleamed as he pulled David aside.

'Come to think of it, there is one way you could show your appreciation of my hospitality tonight, Davey. Drop a good word in that darling's ear for me, hmm? I wouldn't mind taking a better look at those lively green eyes, perhaps over an intimate dinner for two.'

A red haze bled into David's vision. He'd pogo-hop naked down Pitt Street before allowing Jonathon's fangs anywhere near Serena's less experienced stratosphere. She wouldn't stand a chance.

'No can do.' He shook his head. 'Serena's taken.'

The instant that statement shot out, memories of their kiss swirled in his brain, then sparked and sizzled through his system. The promise of fragrant silky skin and satin sheets had become a constant murmur at his ear, but had he jumped the gun in more ways than one? Did Serena have a boyfriend? A couple?

'Taken, eh?' Jonathon's sniff was unmistakably upper class. 'Pity. Although often that doesn't mean much these days.' He called over, 'Cheerio, Serena.'

Turning her back on a picture of America's number-one hip-hop band, Serena sent a smile. 'Guess we'll be in touch over the next few weeks.'

David's hackles rose as a gust of visible speculation filled Jonathon's sails.

'Hmm, guess we will at that.' Jonathon turned to David. 'Booth D is the quickest to set up, but it is rather, shall we say, *cosy*.' He nudged David's ribs and winked as he wheeled away. 'Best of luck, old son.'

CHAPTER FIVE

'DAVID? David, did you hear me?'

Serena reached up and touched his shoulder. David's upmarket loafers shuffled on the parquet floor as he pulled his focus off Jonathon Sturts, who was leaving the room, onto her.

A lock of hair fell over his brow as he rubbed his temple. 'Sorry? What was that?'

'Marissa let us know the booth's ready if we'd like to go through.'

Close by, Marissa waggled a black-polished nail at the adjacent door and headed off. 'This way, people.'

Whatever was behind David's frozen moment, he seemed in tune again now. Smiling, he waved a hand. 'After you.'

In single file, David at the rear, they moved through the connecting doorway and down a carpeted corridor. As they passed gold and platinum awards lining the walls, Serena felt black silk burn a hole through her dress where David's gaze rested.

Imagination had nothing to do with it. The knowledge was as real as the desire she'd seen in his eyes at Jezz's hospital doorway. An hour later, he'd confirmed her suspicions by locking her in an embrace so binding yet weightless, it needed no more than his hands encasing her face and the intensity of his lips to hold her. She'd gone to another place where time and space hadn't been invented. When they'd parted, her brain had refused to work.

He'd let her know, in no uncertain terms, what he wanted. What should be her reply?

As Marissa's boots squelched on Serena swallowed.

David was her boss, a self-assured person of power and means who held her budding career in the palm of his hand. They existed at opposite ends of the spectrum and soon they would be alone. The idea both terrified and excited her.

When Marissa reached sound booth D, she swung open a door to what looked more like a cubby-hole. A black console, patterned with dials and buttons, took up the main wall. Jammed into one corner, a neat pile of music scores sat on the floor. A slow-release vanilla air freshener rested on a ledge beside a stack of CDs.

Marissa slapped her generous thighs. 'This is it.' She scrunched one side of her face. 'Do you need me to hang around and operate the desk?'

David sidled past. Hands resting low on his hips, he cast a glance over the equipment. 'We'll be fine.'

Marissa pushed out a grateful groan. 'When you're done, let yourself out. Security should be around.'

'That's great.' He flicked her a smile. 'You go home.'

As Marissa clopped away Serena ran an eye over the space. Not much room was left now that David filled a major chunk of it.

A vibration deep inside intensified. Her legs trembled. She was aware of every sound, every smell, every object.

Will we kiss again? Will it end there? Or does David regret that crazy moment? Maybe he won't mention it again. It'll be like some of the embarrassing Christmas party incidents I've heard about.

She burrowed in.

At least I'm not jabbering out loud.

The temperature in the cubicle had gone up five degrees by the time they were seated. Her shaky left thigh hovered mere inches from his right.

'Shut the door, Serena.'

She lifted off the seat and swung the door in. The lock clicked, her throat closed, and quicksilver, hot and thick, began to ooze through her bloodstream.

David hunted down two pair of headphones, handed one over, then adjusted his own to a comfortable fit. Punching a button—fiddling with a few slides—he lodged both elbows on the console and propped his chin and its cleft upon the cradle of his knuckles. He sent her a lopsided smile that stirred the puddle of longing welling in her stomach.

He was too close. Or was that not close enough?

'You ready?' he asked.

She inhaled. 'As ready as I'll ever be.'

Seconds later, they were listening to a four-minute version of one very hot tune indeed.

When it came to music—its diversities and extremities—Serena always kept an open mind. For every beat, there was a set of feet. But with this particular composition, who'd need to try? Raunchy, catchy, neither underdone nor overstated, it was one hundred per cent, absolutely, right on the money.

After it played through, she reconnected with her surrounds. She'd hummed aloud with her eyes closed most of the time. From David's amused expression, he didn't mind.

Lines branched from the corners of his eyes as he grinned. 'You like?'

'You couldn't tell?'

It *must* be good to make her forget, even for a moment, that David was sitting this close, close enough to touch.

He chuckled, a deep, rich sound that seeped under her skin and made her stomach muscles flutter.

'When you let loose with that last chorus, it was a pretty decent clue.'

Warmth infused her cheeks. 'Is there more?'

'Would you like more?'

The warmth turned inferno.

Was he talking about the song or playing word games again? She bit the bullet and tested him.

She arched a brow. 'I won't say no.'

He concentrated on the panel and pressed a button. 'Good. Should be at least another half-dozen versions here.'

A knife's cool blade traced over her skin and she straightened. Whatever she'd seen in his eyes, whatever had happened at the Quay, didn't apply in here. Now it was strictly business.

They replaced their headphones and by the third track she'd fallen in love with the music. And she wasn't alone in singing. Usually controlled David Miles was not only bongo-beating his fingers on the desk's edge, he'd joined in a duet that, frankly, was rather impressive. Here again was 'passionate' David, the man she'd glimpsed, touched, tasted. This had to be the tip of the iceberg. Or should that be *volcano*?

The demo ended. When David removed his headphones,

his hair was mussed, and a different, almost animal energy emanated from him. Vanilla faded beneath his fresh masculine scent.

He laid an arm along the back of her chair, brushed her face with his gaze and smiled. 'You're quite the singer, aren't you? Get that from drama class?'

She laughed. He wasn't going to let that die. 'What about you?' A vision popped into her head. 'You must practise in the shower.'

'You've guessed my darkest secret.' His eyes glittered across at her and the room shrank more. Then he chuckled. 'Seriously, I'm lucky Sylvie hasn't howled about it yet.'

Her heartbeat seized. As he reached to drag down a couple of dials the smile slid off her face.

Sylvie? Who the hell was Sylvie? A girlfriend? A live-in lover?

And what about their kiss?

'It's probably a nice accompaniment when she applies her morning make-up.' Serena's words scraped out as her heart emptied, as it had so many times as a teenager—when she hadn't been asked to dance, or had received a C for an assignment she'd had high hopes for.

'Can't be certain—' he turned up a megawatt smile '—but I bet my dog would look pretty silly wearing lipstick.' His chair swivelled. A knee knocked hers and an electric charge shot up her thigh. 'Had her since she was a pup,' he said as the underside of the desk thumped. He winced, shifting more to rub the other knee. 'She's way past that now, though. Sylvie could be mistaken more for a brown bear than a German Shepherd.'

So, not some ravishing redhead, but a *dog*. She loved

dogs! *Adored* them. Still, a question begged to be asked. 'Sylvie's in the bathroom when you take a shower?'

'Usually she's still sprawled out on the bed. Big sook.'

No girlfriend, an animal lover, plus he was a dynamite kisser. The positives for a one-night stand just kept stacking up. But could she pluck up enough courage to give him an opening, an indication that perhaps he should advance?

She settled more into her seat. 'Why don't we listen to the opening track one more time? Maybe I should take some notes.'

David ripped the headphone plugs from the panel. 'It's late.' He flipped down the rest of the dials. 'We should leave.'

What? No, not yet!

She tipped forward to reconnect the cord. 'Couldn't we listen to it just one more time?'

They'd taken care of business, so what about tapping into that other side—the man who had worked her into such a lather, she'd barely been able to form words, let alone explain how his skin on her skin, his tongue on her tongue, had affected her?

David disconnected the cord a second, more definite time. 'No. Afraid not.'

She blinked and eased back in her chair.

The line between his brows, the tension pulling at his jaw...

Rats. He was serious.

But then she saw it.

Most times, David's unruffled exterior gave her little clue. But now his body language spoke to her, loud and clear. The interested angle of his shoulders, the absorbed gleam in his eyes, the pulse pumping in the hollow of his throat.

He wanted to play. He just needed a bigger nod.

A previously untapped sense of recklessness filtered through her as a plan formed and she manufactured a sigh. 'Okay. You're the boss.'

Putting on a beaten face, she raised her hands in surrender. When the spark died from his eyes and he shifted to stand, she banked all on the element of surprise and dived on the cord, then lunged at the panel.

David sprang to life. When his hands caught her wrists, her midsection tightened around a heart-pounding pulse.

'Stevens...?' David couldn't swallow an astonished laugh. 'Damn it, you don't play fair!'

'You know the saying.' Her eyes dared his. 'All's fair...'

For one mad moment, the world stopped spinning and neither one spoke. Instead they held each other's gazes, probing the possibilities, sizing one another up like a couple of duelling gunslingers during a shoot-out in a spaghetti western.

Heart booming, anticipation hanging thick and heavy in the air, she narrowed her eyes, cocked a brow...

And came out shooting!

They scuffled. She had the cord. He wrangled it back. She leapt on him. He tried to block. He was strong, but she was quick. And all the while they laughed.

By the time their energies flagged, one of David's palms lay on Serena's shoulder, the other rested on her chair's armrest. When their laughter petered out, their noses were only inches apart.

His lips were only inches from hers.

Her smile faded, his expression stilled, then shifted. His deep blue eyes focused on hers as his brows drew together. More adrenaline kicked in. Every erogenous zone in her body buzzed on red-hot alert. His study of her was so powerful, her body ached.

Concentrating on her eyes, he squeezed her shoulder.

Last chance to turn back?

From here on in it was clothes peeling off, mutual hunger taking over. Sex. Hot, stormy, shimmering sex. Their relationship would never be the same.

Would she disappoint him in bed? No, she couldn't bring herself to think about that. Maybe he'd want more, but she didn't want an ongoing relationship, and instinct said David's goal there matched her own. They both needed to let go, break free, just for tonight, or they'd *explode*.

David murmured in a valley-deep and careful tone, 'Do you want this?'

Serena's throat was suddenly dry. 'Yes.'

As his gaze drifted lower to settle on her parted mouth a surge of heat blasted through her body. The sensations shot higher as, with an agonizing lack of speed, his palm drifted from its resting place on her shoulder to caress her nape. Any remaining gunpowder flared out of control when he drew her near.

She sensed more than heard the groan rumbling deep in his throat. Tasted more than felt the moist texture of his mouth as it skimmed hers. A kiss so soft, so light, yet it stirred such intense contradictions of sensation. They'd barely touched and it was the most fulfilling intimate contact she'd ever known.

Then his tongue slipped past her lips.

CHAPTER SIX

SERENA had thought their earlier kiss had been fantastic, but nothing compared to this…hot fingers trailing the sweep of her neck, the other hand a brand on her arm, while David's skilful mouth worked patiently to draw her out.

No misunderstandings. It must be true.

She was the most desirable woman alive.

The very heart of her gasped as the pressure of his mouth left hers. Her lips were on fire, her senses, drenched with want.

His eyes were dark. 'At the risk of sounding clichéd…up until an hour ago, I never expected this to happen.'

'Don't worry.' Serena gave him a watery smile. 'I'm pretty sure I wrote the book.'

His gaze intensified. 'Are you seeing anyone?'

She coughed out a laugh. '*No-o-o.*' A sultry redhead flashed to mind. 'Are you?'

His chin tucked in. 'Definitely not.'

That answer both pleased and somehow niggled her. Sounded as if he was unattached and wanted to stay that way, which should be two checkmarks. Right?

That thought evaporated when the side of his hand trailed down over her breastbone and her head rocked back. She closed her eyes and bit down on a sigh as his touch grazed the hidden peak of her breast. The nub tightened and a burn, starting at its tip, swept like a bushfire over her flesh. The base of her stomach quivered at the warm gravelled murmur at her ear. 'I want you.'

A tidal wave crashed and nearly swamped her.

She'd heard those words before. Yesterday in his office had been thrilling enough. But now they held more meaning than she could have dreamed possible. She'd made other wishes. Why had this fantasy so easily come true? What had she done differently? What magical formula had she used?

His teeth raked her chin. 'Did you hear me, Serena?'

She whimpered as her breasts thrust forward and an invisible cord, linking his bite to her centre, pulled tight.

Her eyes drifted open and she grinned. 'You might have to speak a little louder.'

One corner of his mouth came up. 'Louder, huh?'

She thought she might die when his jaw line firmed and he released the clip from her hair, then found the tie of her wraparound dress. A few seconds, one deliberate motion, the dress flipped back and half her bra was exposed. He groaned when he saw the unlined black lace.

'Ms Stevens, is that what you usually wear to business meetings?'

'It is from now on.'

She leaned forward to unbutton his shirt. Inhibition? What was that? Maybe she should have done something like this years ago.

His head dropped to take in her fingers tripping over his buttons. 'You're quick.'

Three to go. 'That's one way to look at it.'

Smile gone, he held both her hands in one of his. Jets of heat flashed up her arms. 'This isn't the best place.'

That yanked her down from the clouds. Heartbeat echoing in her head, she remembered her surroundings. She was in a minuscule booth in the centre of Sydney with her boss, *stripping*.

She nodded. 'You're right.'

They blinked at each other, then the strength of their magnetic fields forced them together again. Their mouths smacked midway.

Hungry now, he peeled the dress from her shoulders down to her elbows. Sick of buttons, she blindly tore his shirt wide open. Kisses at fever pitch, they wriggled closer. Sitting in a cramped space, opposite each other, was less than ideal.

He pushed forward and, hands on her waist, urged her up along with him. Fever spreading, she trembled on weak legs, so aware of his smile even as they kissed.

He slipped the bra straps off her shoulders. A block of heat, his hard chest slid against her till he was on his knees. He massaged her hips so she rocked forward and his face buried in her cleavage. Her head rolled to one side as his tongue swirled and flicked the dip.

His fingers kneaded as he filled his lungs. 'You taste like spring. Fresh air and warm nights.'

She lost her breath. Her hands flexed in his hair, then splayed down toward his nape. It took a moment for the full beauty of those words to truly sink in.

She found a teasing voice. 'That's quite a line.'

'It's true.'

A fingertip rimmed her left bra cup, then eased it down. He dotted soft kisses over the swell till his mouth reached the summit. Nipping, twirling, sucking...his technique drove her mad!

Reaching back with one arm, he shoved at his chair and grunted. 'This is far too awkward.'

Insides smoking, she held his head in place. 'Stifling.'

The clasp at her back snapped open. 'There's just no room.'

Her essence pulsed as she groomed those big bare shoulders beneath his shirt. 'No room at all.'

He grasped the join at the front of her bra. Her breasts spilled out along with her small cry. His dilated pupils lifted to meet hers. 'Maybe you could sit on my lap.'

What untamed creature had overcome her? Sure, she'd wanted one wild night. But she'd envisaged scented sheets, soft pillows, somewhere to lie back and rest after she'd catapulted through the heavens. But that no longer mattered. Decorum didn't exit. She didn't want paradise found as much as paradise *now*.

Shirt half on, David pushed to his feet and heeled off his shoes while she shucked out of a sleeve. Although their eyes were locked, his subtle see-saw movements told her his pants no longer sat upon his hips. He kicked the trousers against the wall, then whipped down her other sleeve. The dress dropped to her ankles. The bra fell too. She was naked but for panties.

His hands looped over her shoulders, ironed her blades, then his arms came around to press her in. The explosion of his heat melted her, inside and out, as his covered erection stabbed her stomach. Her muscles turned marshmallow when his torso ground against her. He feather-kissed her brow and a bonfire erupted at the apex of her thighs.

Lips stirring her hair, he held her close in a subtle intimate dance. 'Is this okay?'

Her heartbeat hammered as light-headedness drew stars before her eyes. 'Okay isn't the word.'

His roaming hands slid over her tailbone, cupped her buns and hauled her in. '*Nice*, then?'

Still recovering from that pre-orgasmic shockwave, she dropped her head against the crisp hair and granite of his chest. She breathed in deeply.

Fix his scent in your mind for ever.

'Nice?' She moistened her lips. 'Let's see…'

She dragged her tongue along his skin as her palms squeezed between their bodies to skim his firm stomach then sweep over those pecs. His grip clenched her bottom as his chest vibrated with an appreciative sound.

'Is that *nice*?' she asked.

His respiratory rate jumped several slots. Still he managed to sound casual. 'Let's say *pleasant.*'

The pads of each index finger stirred the rims of his flat nipples. Her thumbs and fingers came together and—

'Ouch.' But he didn't sound the least bit hurt. She pinched them again just to make sure. 'I would classify that as…' his own fingers slipped under her lower leg elastic and rode the train from back to front '…enjoyable.'

Enjoyable should set her alight with happiness. But that was 'yesterday'. A different woman stood here tonight.

When his wandering fingers dipped in and discovered her moist warmth, her knees buckled. But his other hand on her bottom kept her upright.

He bent and angled his head. 'Hey?' His touch down below deepened, then circled and pressed. 'You all right?'

Dizzy, delirious, drunk with arousal.

'I'm fine…fine…' She didn't want to speak. Her energies were concentrated in other areas, particularly one about to burst into flame.

She tried to drag herself back. It was too soon! She wanted this to last and last.

Grabbing two handfuls of his shirt, she yanked it farther down his back. His hand left her panties so he could release the sleeves.

Almost at the top, she slid back down the climax pole and got her breath. But something bothered her. It was too bright. Dimmer switch? She glanced around. Yes, right behind her.

David brought her close again as the room turned from day to dusk to twilight. Luminous orange spots from the panel and hazy moonbeams emanating from two down-lights…who needed to make love under the stars, just as long as they made love?

His mouth dropped over hers again and they picked up where they'd left off. Stroking, caressing, he amazed her with gentle one minute, rough and playful the next. Heavy breathing, heavier petting. If there'd been a window, it would've been fogged.

David's teeth tugged her earlobe. 'The way I see it, we have three options.' She found the set-cement package between his legs, only half contained inside his Calvin Kleins. He seized her hand and manipulated her fingers to surround him, then hard-pressed in and up and down. '*Oh, dear God…*' She heard him swallow. 'I was saying…three options.'

On tiptoe, she drew her tongue around his Adam's apple. Scratchy. Tasty. 'First option—standing?'

'Yep.'

'And sitting.'

'That's two.'

One more. She thought hard. 'Couldn't be lying down.'

His chuckle was downright evil. 'Maybe I won't shock you with the third option yet.'

Before she could ask, he tipped sideways and felt his way through a search of the console desktop. Should she help? 'What are you looking for?'

'The condom.'

She squeezed him extra hard, but his grunt was all pleasure. He'd taken a condom from his pocket before he'd kicked off his pants? 'You had the foresight to come prepared?' Should she be flattered or miffed? A light bulb went off in her head. Of course, an intelligent, sexually active bachelor would carry one regardless.

He cancelled out both options. 'I bought it from a dispenser at the hospital. Got it!'

Her hand fell away. 'I thought you said you didn't expect this?'

'I *didn't*.' He concentrated on tearing the foil. 'No more than you with your sexy lingerie.'

He had a point.

With lightning-speed precision, he was prepared. In the misty glow he looked like a warrior—a dark, bare-chested, handsome, dominant male. She'd always remember him this way.

When he reached for her again, loved her again, she held onto him as splinters of light built in her mind and her core throbbed and squeezed. Sweet pressure wound tighter as the edge of the world shook and drew near.

When he bounced her up into air, she went with it and scissored her legs around his hips. Holding her with one arm, he ripped her panties' crotch aside and hit his target. The tip filled her, then, as they moved, more and more of his thick, burning length. She couldn't bear it. He felt too good.

Her grasp around his neck slipped. Panic flared up from her toes. But she fell no more than the hammock of his arm allowed. Her fingers dug in. 'Don't let me go.'

He swung her in and nipped her bottom lip. 'Not a chance.'

Slick with perspiration, his muscles clenched as he lifted her slightly, then drove in rock-bed deep. He trembled and groaned while she stilled, quivered then contracted around a blast, so powerful and natural, in that moment she didn't exist but for intensity and instinct.

When the crashing waves ebbed, he was coming back down, too. He shuddered, dragged in a ragged breath, then hummed out a long sigh. As if realizing where he was, he focused on her face and combed away some hair fallen over her eyes. The pad of his thumb traced her lips as his teeth flashed white in the semi-darkness. 'Who said it couldn't be done?'

Who would even imagine such a thing? Especially of her. With *him*. Carly, her best friend, would never believe it. Now it was done, *she* could barely believe it.

He drew her near again. Her hand slipped over his damp chest and steely mound of one shoulder as he kissed the tip of her nose with a tenderness she wanted to bottle. Butterfly kisses next, at her temple, around her jaw and chin. Every time she thought he'd stop, she tingled at another and another. She could have stayed all night.

He finally craned back. 'I'd love to say I could hold you like this for ever.'

Her stomach jumped. She hadn't given a thought to her weight. Not that she was a hulk. She'd made a concerted effort these past years.

She grinned. 'I think you've done exceptionally well.'

His eyes probed hers. 'Guess it's time to land.'

He eased her down.

Ropes of sinew strained and shimmered beneath the moonbeams as he stretched, one arm reaching for the ceiling, the other bent so the bicep bulged. 'Unless you want a rerun, and I'd need to give my thighs a rest for that, we should probably leave.' He collected his shirt, flung over the back of his chair. 'I need to clean up first. There's a bathroom across the hall. Rather fortunate, wouldn't you say?'

As she watched him thread his arms through the sleeves her grin spread wider. 'I wonder if they have a shower?'

He lost interest in missing buttons. 'Want me to check?'

She liked scented baths, but here was a chance to soap up David's back, not to mention his front. He might even serenade her if she was lucky.

But she was forgetting where they were.

A booming knock sounded on the door. Serena's limbs froze as cold blasts of dread snatched her breath away.

Who the hell was that? Oh, God, oh, God. She'd known this was a dumb idea, even if it had been a great idea at the time.

Knock, knock.

David stood stock still. He rasped a whisper across at her. 'Security.'

Oh, God. Security out there. Them naked in here. They'd be tossed in jail for indecent exposure. She could see the look on her father's face now.

David soothed her doom and gloom with a calming smile. He slid past, cleared his throat, upped the light to past halfway and opened the door a fraction. 'Barney, is that you?' he asked in a deep, assured voice. 'It's David Miles.'

She quaked behind the door, eyes closed, really praying this time.

A silence stretched out. 'Mr Miles? It's very late.' Barney sounded more asleep than awake.

'Jonathon let me have this booth for an hour tonight. Got a big campaign to deliver and time's running out.'

'Oh. Sure. Is there anything I can get you?'

'Not right now. I'm about to pack up.'

Serena bit into a finger to stop her teeth chattering.

'Well…okay.' Barney wasn't an easy one to shake. 'I'll be around the traps if you need me.'

'Thanks, Barney. Goodnight now.'

'Yeah. Night, Mr Miles.'

David drew the door in.

Heartbeat galloping, she swept her dress up, then strained her hearing to listen. 'He's still out there.'

David finished buttoning his shirt. 'We just can't hear his footfalls through the insulation.'

After she donned her bra and quickly re-tied the dress, David cracked the door open to peek out. 'I still need to clean up. What about you?'

She always carried tissues. Her panties were ir-redeemable, but she didn't need to wear them. Walking through Sydney without knickers should be chickenfeed compared to the feat of daring she'd performed tonight. Hah! The Mile High Club wasn't so special.

'I'm fine. I'll see you back here—'

'In five.'

She pushed him out. 'Make that two.'

When the door clicked shut, she stepped out of her second-hand panties and blinked around. An odd, wistful feeling washed through her.

So, what happened now? This one-night stand had certainly achieved her short-term goal. Sated, glowing. Frustration and curiosity swept aside. Now it should be back to hard work and on with her career goals. *Onward and upward.*

She fished out a comb from her carryall and wondered.

Did David feel the same way? What would she do if he suggested another night, or *two*? One half of her begged for it—the physical, fanciful part that had found such unprecedented release and raw carnal satisfaction when he'd loved her as she'd never been loved before. But her other half stood firm. That wasn't the plan. One night was one night, but prolonged office affairs got messy.

A stone of doubt dropped into her conscience and she winced.

If she weakened now, set herself up as his regular squeeze, how vulnerable would that leave her? Pillow talk might have its benefits, but what about his respect for her as a capable woman who used her brains, not the bedroom, to get ahead? After funnelling every scrap of time and energy into beating down her self-doubt and achieving at college and beyond, that kind of validation meant everything, including who she was and where she some day hoped to be.

After giving her hair one last run through, she slotted the comb back in her bag. She found her clip and twirled up her tresses, nice and neat.

When he returned, she'd tell him up front, no misunderstandings. This was great, but it was *once*.

A moment later, David walked in with dampened hair, his trousers on and shirt tucked neatly into his belt. She stood when he reached for her hands. He didn't avoid her eyes, but they'd lost their sparkle. His brow was buckled, too.

'We'll take a cab to the car. It'll be quicker that way. But first…' His thumb stroked the back of her hand, but his smile missed reaching his eyes. 'Serena, we need to talk.'

Her stomach knotted and defences shot up.

Did he want to 'let her down gently'? But *she* wanted to do that to *him*. She'd already decided she didn't want a replay. He might hold all the power in a business sense, but she wouldn't allow him to take this decision away from her. If somebody was going to be dropped, it wouldn't be her.

She lifted her chin. 'And our conversation shouldn't take long. I want to say how much I enjoyed tonight.' No need to lie. 'I'll never forget it.'

Not a minute. Not a heartbeat.

He seemed pleased with that. 'Neither will I.' He held her hands tightly. 'Thank you.'

She hid a flinch. 'You don't have to thank me.' It didn't sound right, as if she'd performed some service. And it wasn't like that. Her hands pulled back from his. God, she needed air. These walls were closing in.

She collected her bag resting on the edge of the console. 'It was something that happened…once.'

His brow lowered. 'It doesn't have to be that way.' He half laughed. 'Not that I'm suggesting we do this kind of thing regularly. I've always found high-quality linen and a mattress a good choice.'

Her return smile was bland. That comment only made her think of how many mattresses he might have around the place. She shook her head. 'I don't think so.'

After a long moment, he nodded. 'That's probably best with work and deadlines. That's the priority.' He shucked back his shoulders. 'We don't have to refer to this again, if you'd rather not.'

She hugged her bag as regret spiralled through her. Ten minutes ago they'd been as close as two people could get, bodies sliding, hands searching, fevers climbing. Yet now...

Keeping a tight rein on those emotions, she turned to find the door. 'We really ought to go.'

His hand manacled her wrist and tugged her back. Nerve-endings sparked, her breasts seemed to swell, and that demon desire kicked right back in. Had he decided he wouldn't let her go that easily after all?

His eyes searched hers. 'I just wanted to say—'

Don't say it, don't say it, please say it. 'Yes?'

'Barney's down the end of the corridor. Hope you won't feel too uncomfortable. He won't ask questions.'

Her heart plummeted and smashed at her feet. The muscles in her face collapsed. Yet this was what she wanted. This was the right way, the *only* way she could focus fully on her goals.

First and foremost, he was her boss, expecting her to give her all to this campaign, and rightly so. Beyond that, she planned to work overseas. She'd needed to prove to herself, to her father, to the world, that she could succeed or all those years of hard work would be for nothing. What she and David shared here tonight could never be anything more permanent than a stolen hour.

He swung out the door. 'What time do you expect to be in tomorrow?'

'When do you want me?'

Would he come back with something fun and flirty like, *How about now?*

She watched his back as he stepped out the room. 'Eight a.m. Don't be late.'

CHAPTER SEVEN

SHE affected him. From the start he'd known it. Now he couldn't escape it.

At the head of the polished mahogany table in Miles Advertising's generously sized boardroom, David reclined more deeply into his high-backed chair and drank in that shining fair hair and smooth clear voice. A second later, he bit his inside cheek at the push of longing compounding in his gut.

Serena was addressing Josh Winton, the creative director, and Burt Foggle, copy, regarding the print campaign she and Jezz McQade had put together. And wasn't she doing a brilliant job? Neither nervous nor uncertain—not in the least. She'd taken her lessons seriously. If he hadn't known better, he'd guess she'd been liaising on this level for years.

In truth, it was just over four weeks since he'd awarded her the position of second-in-charge of the *Hits* campaign—thirty-one days and nights since their episode at Mixem Studios. And from that time to this, David hadn't been able to get Serena out of his mind.

The taste of her mouth and body hadn't faded from memory. The soft texture of her skin was still clear in his head. The sex had been unbelievable. Tender. Playful. More exciting than he'd ever known. Against his better judgment, he'd been ready to go back for more.

But Serena had made it clear: it had been a one-time offer only. He commended her on making the right decision—she was even more mature than he'd first thought—but, deep down, he hadn't been happy about it. And that was scary.

He wasn't stupid. He knew the signs. The way his body heated when he saw her. The way his mind turned off when he recognized her smile or her laugh as she walked into the room. He was riding a fast train, hurtling towards a station called 'danger of falling in love.'

With an *employee*.

He thought of Olivia Roundtree and cringed.

Smart and sassy, Olivia had been hired when his agency was small and his hopes for it were shiny new. Still wet behind the ears, he'd been eager to prove himself and she'd given him confidence, in more ways than one. When he'd promoted her, she'd done an adequate job in the office, but that had taken a backseat to the way her adventurous nature had ignited his libido. They had been a couple, he'd thought a happy one. Then one day out of the blue she'd upped and announced she was jumping a jet and leaving the country. She'd wanted to find herself, learn and grow. No hard feelings.

Yeah, right.

If that weren't enough, she'd left smack in the middle of an important campaign they'd been working on together. Both his agency and heart had been sacrificed for the sake of what he'd then called love. But this recent scenario possessed an even sharper double-edge.

Removing the Montblanc hitched behind one ear, David

furrowed his brow and tapped Serena's A-grade print proposal with the pen.

If he decided to push it and pursue an intimate relationship, which he could *taste* he wanted it so bad, and Serena agreed, what happened if she somehow screwed up the campaign? There were numerous ways a blunder could still happen before Jezz was back on deck. How would that affect his relationship with his clients? With his colleagues in the industry?

They'd say he was driven by his head, and not the one on his shoulders. Everyone would recall how he'd been just as brainless when he'd hedged all his bets on Olivia and had lost so badly on that hand. He'd been young and foolish the first time. What excuse would he have now?

Then again, if this campaign went belly up, he wouldn't have to worry about gossip. He'd be out of business and this time there'd be no second chance.

'Is that okay with you, David?'

He started. Rather than admit to being on another planet, he rocked forward, grunting along the lines of, 'Sure, Serena. That's fine.'

He fell back into his previous train of thought, his gaze washing over her bewitching face then body as she scooted back her chair to round the table and continue relaying her top-notch ideas.

He sponged up the keen sparkle of her eyes, the slim energetic line of her limbs, the way those low-waist dress pants hugged her shape as though they'd been stitched with only her hips in mind. A glimpse of her tanned tummy was visible below a stretchy white blouse. Every so often a belly bauble glittered as though winking at him. Normally he'd consider that too younger generation for his taste. Yet on Serena it only served to complement one highly irresistible package.

Then there was her breezy manner. That tinkling laugh. The mask of concentration when she lodged a pencil between her teeth and stared at the floor while considering some important point. How her eyes shone, as they did now, with a passion he craved to know intimately again. It made him want to sweep her up, escape somewhere, and forget everyone and everything but her. Her embrace, her abandon, her hands clasping his neck as they both spiralled up into glittering space.

The death grip on his pen eased.

The answer was really very simple. He needed to kiss Serena Stevens. No, more than kiss her. Bed her. Have her again. Unwrap the clothes from her body and make uncensored love to her flesh and to her mind. If not as an ongoing relationship, which clearly was best, then just one more time.

He'd find a way to make certain that was enough.

He didn't realize the meeting had finished. As people milled past he pushed out of his seat to catch Serena.

She gazed over at him with her usual dimpled smile as they moved together out the room, but something subtle about that expression had changed and he couldn't quite put his finger on what. Maybe it was because he saw her differently now. Maybe it was because *she* did.

He straightened his tie. 'Have you spoken with Jezz this morning?' They only talked shop these days. Safer than innuendo, certainly, but not nearly as much fun. 'Will she make it to the launch tomorrow night?'

The promotional launch of *Hits* would be held at David's large, some might say palatial, home. The two-storey Mediterranean-style dwelling, complete with all the trappings of luxury, was perfect for his company's high-profile occasions, like tomorrow evening's soirée.

Arms full of folders, gaze dead ahead, Serena moved down the corridor. 'Jezz's leg is still giving her trouble. She's on antibiotics.'

'We won't see her tomorrow night, then?'

'I'm hoping so, but maybe not.'

'Which means you'll have to take front seat there as well.'

'You don't think I'm up to it?'

Since the booth incident, Serena's attitude had changed. More assertive and confident. Great. But sometimes, like now, she could sound defensive or annoyed. About their night together? No reason to be—she'd enjoyed herself as much as he had. And she'd been the one to set the one-time-only rule, even when he'd let her know he was open to the suggestion of seeing her privately again.

As to her handling the launch responsibilities, naturally he'd expect her to be nervous about taking the lead in front of hundreds of inquisitive strangers. But he'd be there to support her.

'You'll do fine,' he assured her. 'The crowd will lap you up.' Her smile could be more convincing, so he added, 'The guest list is impressive. Reviewers, agents, reporters, recording executives, international acts visiting the country. You've done a great job getting it together.'

Serena simply nodded.

Was she *that* daunted by the idea of playing hostess to the *crème-de-la-crème* crowd? He wouldn't have been surprised a month ago, but she seemed to have grown so much since then.

She shifted the folders in her arms as they passed the water cooler. 'Will Rachel be there?'

He nodded. 'My other clients would expect it.' An ugly thought struck. 'Has she been behaving herself?'

No reports of her jealousy over Serena being awarded the campaign had leaked back to him thus far. Even given her bouts of brilliance, his judgment must have been in the john the day he'd given Rachel Bragg that five-year contract. Far too temperamental. He didn't know a single person in the company who got along with her, including him. He'd give his lawyers another call. That woman had an ego the size of China, but surely if he offered a big enough cheque she'd bow out.

'I can handle Rachel,' Serena told him.

David reached to scoop the folders from her arms. She hesitated a moment at the contact, before giving in to hand them over.

'Anything I need to know before the launch kicks off?' he asked.

Serena shook out her arms as she strolled beside him. 'A few catering details need sorting out. But other than that, all systems are go.'

'Good, good.' David nodded over, a lame grin stuck on his dial, when all he wanted to do was bury his face in the sweeps of hair spilling over her shoulders and nuzzle the perfumed slope of her neck. His gaze skied down the length of one toned, tanned arm. Already he could taste the honeyed landscape of her skin.

For the hundredth time he asked himself: how did Serena feel about him now? They'd never discussed the booth incident. They'd agreed it was best. But more and more he felt compelled to break the silence. Beneath this new polished exterior, was she in as much torment as him?

He followed Serena through into an office originally

intended for Jezz. She gestured to the credenza and he placed his bundle next to a whirring fax machine, which was busy spitting out a string of quotes from an exclusive model agency.

'You've worked hard these past weeks.' He slapped any grit from his hands and faced her. 'The weekend will be full on. Why don't you take Monday morning off? Have a facial.' *Or come to bed with me.*

She seemed shocked. 'I can't do that.' Her gaze flew around the room to take in the mountains of prints and copy and scripts banked up in each corner. 'I've got too much to do.'

He'd closed the distance between them. But she walked around him to sit at her desk.

He'd been dismissed? His back straightened. He wasn't ready to leave. 'I was about to organize a coffee? Want one?'

With that almost-smile, she glanced up from the report she studied. 'I don't drink coffee.'

Really? 'Why don't I know that?' He lived on the stuff.

She shrugged. 'You never asked.'

He crossed the room and hooked a leg over the corner of the desk closest to her chair. She swivelled left to face him…to let him know she wasn't intimidated? That couldn't be right.

He smiled inside.

Or, to show she could manage the restraint as well as he could.

He jerked his chin at her desk. 'Then what's the mug for?' He swept it up and read the logo painted in pink funky letters across the ceramic white. '*Go Girl*, huh?' *Cute.*

'I've had it a while.' She took it from him and set it back down 'Water. I drink lots of water throughout the day.'

He raised his brows. *Good for her.* 'What do you drink at night?' A subtle tease? So shoot him. He'd missed their word games. Didn't she?

'Chardonnay…' she blinked '…with red soda.'

He swung his leg. 'I have the occasional beer.'

Her nose screwed up. 'I hate beer.'

'Nothing better when a big game's on.'

'Football?' He nodded. Her gaze didn't falter. 'I hate football.'

His leg stilled. She was determined to prove her point. They were different. Incompatible? But didn't opposites attract? He leant the barest margin forward. 'What *do* you like?'

Her cheeks pinked up, but her expression didn't budge. 'I like my work.'

'I know that.' He wouldn't be put off. 'What else?' *I know at least one thing.*

Her gaze wavered. She turned back to her desk and started scribbling a lengthy note on a spreadsheet. 'I like Thai food.'

'So do I. Pad Thai noodles. But it's got to have lots of chilli.'

'I don't like it hot.'

'I think you do.'

She shot up from her desk. The chair flew back. Her chest went in and out in shallow little breaths. Red patches crept up her neck. 'I have a lot to get done.'

His gaze swept over her as he took his time standing. He shouldn't interfere with her focus; the quality of her input meant as much to him as her.

But this wasn't over, and today he'd decided he wanted her to know it. They'd made love once and catastrophe hadn't befallen either one of them. He could, and would, have her in his arms again. Though she wouldn't say, to his very bones he knew she wanted that, too.

He headed for the door. 'We'll talk later.'

Halfway out into the corridor she called him back. 'I almost forgot. Yesterday I spoke with a Linda Marley, a record producer.'

Turning back to listen, David drew the pen from his shirt pocket and clicked the top in and out.

'We've bumped into each other a few times these past weeks,' she explained, 'and Linda's come up with a great idea to stage a mini auction tomorrow night.'

The pen stopped clicking. 'Go on.'

'We could give out numbers and have people bid on, say, a half-dozen items. The money could go to flying an out-of-state viewer to the première show as a special guest. Give them accommodation, limo service, the whole deal. The publicity would make a sensational spread.'

As usual, David admired her enthusiasm and vision—that was why he'd hired her for this job in the first place. However, 'A lot of organization would need to go into something like that before tomorrow night. Do you have the time?' He doubted it. She was up to her eyeballs already.

'I can try. Linda said she'll give me a hand.'

He tugged an ear. 'Have you spoken to Jezz about this?'

'Not yet.'

David thought it through. If Serena could pull it off, the publicity would be a nice bonus. However, he didn't want her to jeopardize the other pots she had on boil. He could trust Jezz's opinion on this one to know exactly where Serena was at and whether this idea was feasible.

'Run it by her and if Jezz thinks it'll fly—' he turned to leave '—you got me, top to bottom.'

'I couldn't ask for anything more.'

What?

He spun back, but her head was buried again in paper-work. Intrigued more than ever, he moved down the corridor towards his office.

Before his night with Serena, he'd had a dry spell. Good sex was better than fine, but, as well as the sizzle, he missed the comfort of an intimate partner, speaking quietly in the darkness with someone cradled in his arms, the company of soft feminine breathing only slightly out of sync with his own. But not just any woman.

It had to be Serena.

He swept into his office and slammed the door.

Was he fooling himself? Would one more night be enough? Tomorrow he planned to find out.

CHAPTER EIGHT

RECLINED in a canvas chair on Jezz McQade's balcony, Serena tried her best to look unconcerned at news that left her a little faint.

'I'm so sorry, hon. Truly I am.' Jezz tipped back in her chair and drove frustrated fingers through that flurry of red hair. 'I wish this blasted leg would hurry up and mend, the doctor says it doesn't look good.'

Gaze drifting from the cast to a panoramic view of the city, Serena processed the information. She'd hoped like crazy Jezz would be well enough to go to the launch—that way her stomach could stop churning like a cement mixer as she thought about tomorrow night.

Serena felt a pat on her shoulder. She looked away from the sunset to find Jezz's warm expression.

'If I possibly could, you know I'd go.' Jezz gave the shoulder a rub, then sat back and growled. 'If this leg weren't so bloody stubborn and my medication didn't put elephants to sleep—'

Serena surrendered to a grin. Jezz always made her smile, which was a big reason they worked so well together. There'd been late nights and tight schedules, biting nails and frantic phone calls. But, mainly, these past weeks had been fun. Jezz had let her know in lots of ways that she'd developed a soft spot. Jezz had become something more than a friend to Serena as well.

Unable to get comfortable, Jezz shifted in her chair, then realigned the cushion at her back. 'I know you'll be sensational tomorrow night. Just like you've been all along. You've done a fantastic job. David agrees. He thinks you're pretty special.'

Chest growing tight, Serena averted her eyes again.

Of course she'd said nothing to Jezz about the scene at Mixem's. Would she even be able to put into words how the experience had affected her?

Once she'd made up her mind to fulfil her one-night stand fantasy, her course had been set. Making love with her boss in a veritable cupboard at a respected inner-city address had to be the most reckless, impulsive things she'd ever done, by a mile. And she'd regretted not one moment of it.

Until they'd dressed and it had been time to leave. Then the doubt monsters had really come out to play.

She'd decided to stick to her plan: one time only, get David and her sexual frustrations out of her system, then concentrate on work, on continuing her journey to fulfil her destiny. But her hackles had shot up when she'd thought David would beat her to the punch in saying there wouldn't be a next time. *Then* he'd turned things around and suggested more sex on the side. He'd mentioned mattresses and from that point on she hadn't known if she wanted to forget it ever happened or beg him to take her again.

She still didn't know.

Serena gazed out over the surrounding skyscrapers. Way above the rest stood the Centrepoint Tower's golden turret.

Its spire reached up to wispy clouds that brushed a tranquil blue sky rimmed in the west by yellow and rose.

Serena sighed.

What was David doing now?

Jezz's chair grated on the tiles and Serena snapped back. Crutches in place, Jezz hopped through the doorway, which led to the apartment's main room.

'Come inside,' she called. 'There's something we still need to organize for tomorrow night.'

Serena pushed to her feet. She'd thought she'd seen to everything. Though she'd never admit it, she'd been so busy all week her energy levels were dragging their feet. But this was by far the most important task she'd been given. If the promotional launch of the *Hits* programme was a success, she'd have proven herself beyond doubt to not only David but also herself. She'd have an excellent addition to her résumé when she headed overseas.

Her stomach clenched.

She held her gold heart and moved from the balcony into the apartment.

Anxiety. Still happened sometimes when she thought about leaving home. But her dream *would* happen. It had to, or she'd feel as though she'd screwed up. Just as she'd screwed up so many times through school and fallen short in her dad's eyes; he was always on to her about doing things his way.

But for now she needed to concentrate on proving herself here.

'Hon?' Jezz and her crutches stood at the far end of the room. 'Can you come over here? I have a devil of a time lowering my behind onto this couch.'

When Jezz was comfortable, she patted the cushion

beside her. 'What's that I always see you wearing around your neck?'

'It's a gift from my mother.' Serena's heart squeezed as it always did whenever she spoke about her. 'She died a few years back. She said it was to remind me that I could reach the stars if I tried.'

Jezz looked from the heart into Serena's eyes. 'That's about the loveliest thing I've ever heard. Whenever I told my mother I wanted to sing in Vegas, she'd brush the top of my head and tell me to go feed the chickens.' She chuckled.

'But you *did* sing in Vegas.'

Jezz's eyes flashed. 'And I dazzled 'em too. Just like you're going to dazzle every single person there tomorrow night.' She clapped her hands and rubbed them together. 'So, you must have a stunning outfit lined up. Tell me about it.'

Serena froze. She'd been flat out, but why had she not thought of a dress until now? Her mind ran through her walk-in. Smart-casual, business, grunge, weekend… Her heart began to thump. 'I must have *something*.'

Jezz thought for a moment, then dived on the side-table phone. 'Never fear. Your fairy godmother is here.'

Fairy godmother. The title suited her, in a very contemporary kind of way. But, 'Who are you calling?'

Jezz placed her call and waited. 'All That boutique.'

'The exclusive place in the lobby?' Serena shook her head. 'I can't afford anything from there.'

Jezz simply smiled. 'Hello. Jezz McQade from Room 2810. I need something in a size—' she flung an appraising glance over Serena's frame '—eight for a black-tie affair tomorrow evening. What have you got that will leave three hundred people gobsmacked?'

Serena shook her head faster. A handbag from All That would blow her budget, let alone a gown.

'No price limit,' Jezz said into the receiver. 'Breathtaking is the only requirement.' She winked at Serena. 'You'll be up here in fifteen minutes with a selection?' She checked her watch. 'Done. Mind doing me another favour? Make a booking with the beautician next door for two-thirty tomorrow afternoon. Shampoo, blow-dry, manicure, pedicure. The works!'

'Get them back,' Serena begged as Jezz hung up. 'Next you'll be calling a limo. I can't afford it.'

'You're representing Miles Advertising and you're going to look the part. And don't worry about the bill. I'll square it with David. He'll be delighted.'

Serena thought of how David wanted to be kept up to date with expenses. He might have slept with her, but business was business. 'I'm not so sure he will be.'

'Well, I am.'

Serena's gaze shot up from the floor. 'What makes you say that?'

Jezz wiggled her fingers and Serena helped her up and onto her crutches. 'Because he's interested, and not just in your advertising abilities.'

Serena watched Jezz hop and swing over to the fridge. 'You know that?'

Jezz found and uncapped a bottle of sparkling apple juice. 'I also know there's been contact between you two.' The intended meaning of the word 'contact' was made clear by her tone.

Serena crept closer. 'How do you know?'

Was it etched in her forehead? Had she spoken in her sleep? How *much* did Jezz know? That after a sizzling night, David had agreed to never raise the issue again? His professional attitude towards her afterwards had made her respect him. His personal disinterest had also made her want to cry or slap his face.

Jezz poured two glasses and offered Serena one. 'I know because his chest expands if either of us mentions your name, and when I ask you to speak with him about something, your cheeks turn the colour of crushed berries.'

Serena felt those berries now. 'Doesn't mean anything's happened.'

Jezz wasn't buying. 'Am I wrong?'

She buckled. 'No.'

And today, after four weeks on the wagon, David had started with his teasing again, word games, meaningful lidded looks that ignited flash fires in her veins.

They'd agreed never to discuss it, but was that best? She didn't have the least idea what she'd say, but more and more she needed to say something. Something smug or hurtful or possibly desperate. And that was what she was more afraid of than anything. If he brought up their clandestine night, she'd either start rambling and embarrass herself. Or jump on him and embarrass herself. Neither option was good.

'My best advice for tomorrow's party is—' Jezz raised her glass '—just have fun.'

Serena took a long sip.

As long as I don't 'fun' myself into trouble and out of a job.

The following day, Serena rubbed her palms down the sides of her jeans and followed Gilbert, David's butler, as they walked from the mansion down a wide slate path lined with mint-green pines.

This afternoon she'd made doubly certain that everything was in place for tonight's promotional launch of the *Hits* campaign. Several times during these past weeks, when she'd known David was at the office, she'd come to his home to prepare. She needed to ensure that the glittering line-up of guests was impressed, but more so that the all-important sponsors were dazzled.

The situation was similar to a leading sportswear company wanting to know that the tennis or football star they sponsored was receiving the very best exposure, as well as assurance that their advertising dollars were handled by people with class, pizzazz and first-class initiative. With Jezz's help, Serena aimed to do just that.

Silver-haired Gilbert, who was dressed in chinos and a patterned open-necked shirt, spoke over one shoulder to her. 'Mr Miles insisted I bring you to him before you left the grounds today. Perhaps we could organize some bathers and you could join him for a dip?'

Further down the slope, David pulled his athletic body through the crystal-blue water of a fifty-metre pool. He flipped at the far end, then re-emerged to freestyle leisurely back.

Water. David. Minimum of clothes.

'Not this time, Gilbert.' The idea was way too tempting.

A flock of king parrots winged-in overhead to land in a grevillia grove the other side of a spectacular floral garden clock. Beyond the cliff face, the harbour entertained a fleet of sailing yachts. Enormous entry gates, imposing Mediterranean-style home, tennis court, pristine lawns…

When she'd first seen this place, she'd almost fallen over. David wasn't merely wealthy, he must be a multi-

multimillionaire. Where had all this money come from? Had his company earned him this kind of fortune? Mansions and grounds such as these existed in movies. Her two-bedroom Manly apartment was a cubby-hole compared to this.

She held her stomach when it kicked.

If she didn't mention the C.H. word, or start rambling or fantasizing, she should manage to keep her clothes on and everything would be fine.

When they reached the pool area's sandstone pavers, Gilbert bowed off and David kicked up out from the pool. He walked over, dark hair dripping and powerhouse of muscles glistening in the warm sunshine.

He snatched a white towel off the back of a chaise and ruffle-dried his hair as he joined her.

Memories from the booth swooped upon her, but she forced her gaze away from those shoulders to his eyes and spoke first. 'I was making a final check for tonight. Gilbert said you wanted to see me.'

He looked so different in these surrounds. Even more assured, more attractive. Every part of him seemed to be highlighted…his square chin, his height, the scar on his brow that she'd kissed so many times that night. Of course, it didn't hurt that he was almost naked.

He raked back his hair. 'Everything okay?'

She sucked in a quick breath but kept a cool face. 'Appears to be. All the pieces for the auction are in place, which was the main reason for the visit.'

'I meant is everything okay with you?' He moved forward. She moved back. He held her gaze but didn't smile or grin as he wrapped the towel around his washboard waist. 'You seemed rather nervous yesterday. Or upset.'

Yes, she was nervous about tonight. But she'd been more nervous about the way he'd looked at her. The things he'd said. Or hadn't said. And she'd been upset because she hadn't the least idea how to handle it, as if her confidence had slid back ten years, and that frustrated the hell out of her. How brainless to let slip her own play on words, though she hadn't dared look up to see his reaction.

David gestured towards a square table and two chairs. The close proximity of all that raw sexuality worried her, but for now she couldn't escape.

He pulled out her chair and she took her seat. 'I admit I am a little anxious about tonight,' she said.

'I was about to call Gilbert for lunch. Have you eaten?' Sitting opposite, he collected a handset resting on the tabletop. He punched a button and put the receiver to his ear. 'I ordered Caesar Salad. Or would you like something heavier? I usually have a big breakfast.'

She blinked at him. Was he interested more in what she had to say or fine dining?

She waved for him to put the phone down. 'I'm really not hungry.' A question popped into her mind. 'Do you often ask poor Gilbert to trudge down that hill with your food?'

What was it like to have someone serve and cook and clean and answer the door for you? She couldn't imagine. Her mother had always laughed about how wonderful it would be to have a maid.

'I eat most times at the office or at business dinners. Gilbert likes to spoil me when I'm home. But if he's the only one in, I normally jog up and he meets me at the door.'

A butler, every luxury, real estate worth a fortune. 'Where on earth did you get all this money?'

She bit her lip, then released it. If that was too direct,

too bad. Who wasn't curious about the people who lived in big mansions and drove expensive cars?

'My parents were rather well off.'

Serena fell back in her chair. 'Well off or loaded?'

He sucked down a breath. 'Loaded pretty much sums it up. My father was the biggest, toughest barrister of his day. Commanded outrageous sums for his time. He socked everything into real estate, stock market or gold, depending on the cycle. By the time he died, he was up there with the wealthiest men in the country.'

'Which makes you one of the wealthiest now.' That *was* being a snoop. But the idea of this much *everything* astounded her.

He sat back too and laced his hands behind his head. Serena groaned under her breath. Muscle on top of muscle, a perfectly sculptured chest—big, bronze and beautiful. If he'd struck that pose to get a reaction, he'd definitely got one.

His right pec flexed as he got more comfortable. 'My brother and I were left financially well off after our mother passed away. But a lot was given to help relatives in England. Quite a deal more was left to charity.'

'That's incredibly generous.'

David lowered his arms, darn it.

'Dad was a tough old guy, but thoughtful too. And fair. Deep down his heart was the softer than my mother's. She taught ballet to the up-and-coming best. I've never met anyone more disciplined.' He swatted some gnat or other on his shoulder. 'Are you thirsty?' He collected the phone again. 'Water, or maybe a wine and soda?'

He was making a real effort. To seduce her? Did she want to be seduced? No! She'd already decided. No innuendo, plus no sex, equalled no embarrassing situations like skulking out from Mixem's minus her underwear, or jeopardizing his respect for her and thus her position. And she needed that respect—this position—to help get her where she wanted to go.

Still, what woman wouldn't want to wrap herself around a man like him?

While he spoke to Gilbert, she slid a glance over his body, still damp from the swim, then the strong, chiselled planes of his face. Powerful, rich, an expert lover, and that was when he was standing up. Her pulse rattled as she imagined his repertoire given the bonus of more space and resources.

He set down the phone and nudged back his chair. 'I'll just run up and get the drinks.'

She inhaled and pushed herself to her feet.

'I really ought to go.' She almost said sorry but bit it off. She didn't want him to know just how sorry she was. 'I have an appointment at half past two.'

He didn't say anything, just looked, but she could read his eyes. They said he wanted her to forget the appointment. He wanted her to stay. But if she stayed she couldn't trust herself, and after yesterday she knew she couldn't trust him.

Could he read *her* eyes? That she'd love nothing better than to run her hands over those arms, trail moist kisses along his sun-warmed olive skin? But she couldn't be sure that twice wouldn't turn into three times, then four. She didn't want to have an affair with David. She didn't want to look forward to the next time.

She didn't want to get attached.

He looked her up and down, blinked twice, then turned away. 'I'll get a robe and see you out.'

She almost had to sit down again. His face had been

hard, but she'd seen his disappointment. Why did this have to be so complicated?

She wandered over as he vanished through the doorway of a white block pool house, which was big enough to be a house in its own right. Checking the time, she moved up to the door. She really ought to hurry if she was going to—

David was standing at the far end of the room, back to her. He'd just stripped off his swimwear.

Her throat closed and heartbeat exploded as she stared at that broad back, long thick legs, tight centrefold buns. This was male animal perfection.

When he tossed the swimmers on a wet floor next to a shower, he must have caught a glimpse of her out of the corner of his eye.

A terrible, wonderful thrill flew through her. When her lungs burned, she remembered to breathe. Through tunnel vision she watched him slowly face her, then move with long casual strides her way.

Assured, purposeful—the gait of a hunter. And she was his prey. She didn't know whether to run for her life, play possum or enjoy being eaten.

When he stopped, she felt as if she stood in the shadow of a mountain. His arms gathered her in and any remaining moral fibre seeped away. His hand funnelled through one side of her hair and tugged. Her neck arced back and she was faced by the full force of it—his magnetism and his will.

He reached between them and dragged down her jeans' zipper, then pressed on her back with his other hand till her breasts met his bare chest. His mouth found the shell of her ear. She trembled when he told her, 'This time I won't ask.'

CHAPTER NINE

ONLY hours after making love to Serena, David stood in the centre of his home's grandiose foyer—colossal chandelier overhead, upbeat music playing, the first of his guests arriving for the big event.

He should be pumped about it. Tonight would play an integral role in keeping that client happy. But the bigger part of him couldn't wait to get the crowd out so he and Serena could test his bed in the master suite. The shower in the pool house had been sensational, *twice*.

'One more time' hadn't been nearly enough.

Resplendent in black tuxedo, Greg Harold from a rival agency had arrived with his vivacious wife five minutes earlier. Recording agent guru, Snork Merril—strange name, strange man—had made his much-heralded appearance with partner, Phil Daniels. Over a hundred guests so far, some looking as though they'd come in fancy dress, others straight from a rave party. And still no Serena.

He was beginning to worry. All sorts of scenarios were taking shape in his mind. She was held up at work, injured in a car accident.

Boarding a plane.

His stomach muscles contracted.

In fact, he couldn't wait any longer. He wouldn't settle till he dialled her cell and she picked up. He'd just check the entrance a final time.

He turned in time to see *the witch* swoop in through his front door.

'Hello, Rachel.' His smile was thin but polite. 'Glad you could make it.'

She sashayed up with her usual air, then smoothed the cobalt-coloured fabric of her tight cocktail number. Her ebony eyes said, *Don't feed me that crap; this should be my launch to run,* while her vocal cords chimed, 'I'm so glad to be here.' She flung her brunette waves and an unimpressed look around. 'Where's Serena?'

'She'll be here soon. A few last-minute details to attend to.'

Rachel looked scandalously pleased. 'At this late hour? I hope she has things under control…' she paused for effect '…for everyone's sake.'

After a manufactured start, she waved an arm in greeting. 'Sedwick Rottell!'

A middle-aged broadsheet editor, sporting a silver goatee and unlaced sneakers, rotated his hand in the air as if he were royalty.

Rachel set off. 'Good luck, David. Let me know if you need any help.'

David mumbled under his breath, 'Not likely.'

'Pardon?'

At the voice at his back, he spun around. One elbow slammed into something warm and soft. Both hands shot out to blindly steady the situation. They caught Serena, who stood, face pinched, before him. She was rubbing an upper arm.

An impulse grabbed him. He thrust his hands into his pockets to keep them from doing things he might regret.

Not now. Manners first. Lovin' later.

Her expression warmed. He tipped towards her and murmured, 'You make me hot.'

'And you made me late. I wanted to be extra early.'

'Well, now you're extra clean.'

She play-slapped his chest, then began talking, but he was engrossed drinking in the picture of a woman who'd never looked more dazzling. Silky hair flipped up in a glittering hairdo, an exquisite full-length gown—pale pink, hugging but sophisticated—and a face that was a hundred times more beautiful than any model's. He was one very lucky man.

Serena's words filtered through to his conscience.

'There was the salon appointment, which I was late for—' she narrowed her eyes '—thanks to you. It took for ever. And Jezz organized for a private fashion parade yesterday, but this afternoon they sent the wrong size. Oh, and that's the other thing I wanted to talk to you about—'

He placed a finger close to her mouth and she shut up. 'Whatever it is, it has to wait. You have a launch party to manage.' Her smile didn't so much widen as bloom when he braced a hand on her lower back to guide her toward the adjoining room. He nodded at the curious faces they passed. What were they thinking?

Who was this angel David Miles was with? Was she as intelligent as she was lovely? How long would she hang around?

David's breathing hitched. His hand went to his throat as he cleared it.

He wouldn't allow that black thought. He didn't want to think about the answer.

He slid over a glance and was comforted by the depth of those dimples. 'Everything's under control.' He smiled. 'But you knew it would be.'

Serena clutched a purse to her breast, her eyes shining more brightly than tomorrow morning's dawn. He'd missed that expression. Hadn't seen it for weeks. When she smiled at him like that, it made him feel invincible. As if he could never be more complete. As if everything he had now was all he'd ever need.

Did he ever want to let that feeling go?

He did know he wanted to continue seeing Serena. If this afternoon was any indication, he guessed she wouldn't say no. They could go from there. See where this led them.

Her eyes skated around the room. 'Everything does appear to be going extremely well.'

The prepared stage, the clouds of quaver-shaped balloons, the city-lights view beyond the terrace doors. Pretty much perfect. Better yet were their guests' expressions, the way everyone enjoyed the same heightened sense of anticipation.

Serena whirled on him, suddenly alarmed. 'I forgot! I have to check the sound system. The technician was concerned the cables might not—'

'Taken care of.' David steered her towards a waiter's tray and selected two flutes of champagne. 'Relax while you can.'

In a minute they'd both have to take care of business, but he wanted just a little time to reflect on their soul-lifting afternoon, possibly swap a couple of soap stories. Maybe talk a little about the immediate future.

A woman with a martini, dirty blonde hair and a black trouser suit butted in. 'Hey, Serena! This is *fa-a-an*-tastic. You've got the whole damn town here.'

Serena beamed and hugged her. 'It is kind of special, huh?'

'David Miles.' He offered his hand, which the woman shook quite vigorously. 'And you are...?'

'Linda Marley.'

Serena explained. 'Linda was the lady who had the auction idea, remember?'

'Oh, right. Should go really well.' David cupped Serena's elbow. 'Unfortunately, Linda, Serena and I have some last-minute details to attend to, but I'm sure she'll be available to talk with you later.'

Serena turned to him. 'David, would you excuse us for a moment? I'd like to go over the details for the auction one last time.'

This Linda woman didn't hesitate. She didn't look back either. 'Lead the way. Serena, you look fabulous...'

David clenched his jaw and let his disappointment fade before he headed into the crowd.

Should he expect anything less? Serena was the one who'd put all this together. Was the one to ask questions of, to share a drink with, to applaud. Tonight she was running the show and she needed room to do it.

He waved down a friend who worked in radio and crossed to join him, but even as they chatted about old times he still thought of Serena.

She was coming up in the world. He needed to give her enough line or she wouldn't continue to rise. If Serena grew too fast, got over-confident and started making doubtful decisions, then would be the time to haul her back. But that was unlikely. She listened to him, respected his decisions. That wouldn't change.

He mingled with acquaintances and chatted with a few close friends. In good spirits, one hour and twenty conversations later, David caught sight of Serena again. She was talking—laughing—with someone…he couldn't quite see who.

Her companion stood out of sight behind a pillar. That was fine. Serena was the person he wanted to admire. Something about her was so special. She aroused him, beyond what any human being should have to endure.

He didn't plan on suffering. They'd work something out, because this awareness went past anything he'd known before. She made him feel as he hadn't done in years. Back before Olivia or his father's illness to when he was young and believed one day he'd fly jets.

Serena moved away from the pillar. Her companion joined her. The glass almost shattered in David's hand, he squeezed it so tight.

Jonathon Sturts, and he was dropping a kiss on Serena's hand.

After a final word, Jonathon sauntered away. A coal burned a hole in his gut as David accepted Jonathon's handshake a moment later.

'Davey, old son. I've been speaking with your beautiful hostess.'

He gave a thin smile. 'So I see.'

'She certainly is a gem.' Jonathon sipped what smelled like straight bourbon. 'Is it true she put this together while organizing all the other aspects of the *Hits* campaign?'

David's mask eased. 'She's a talented lady.'

Jonathon regarded Serena again, this time with increased interest. 'And quite young.'

'She's twenty-four.' *Almost twenty-five*.

Jonathon pitched David a meaningful look. 'Experienced?'

David frowned. 'What do you mean by that?'

A curious light shone from behind those feline eyes. 'You don't have your finger in her pie, do you, Davey?'

Although his pulse rate doubled, David didn't blink. 'That is none of your business.'

The ice in Jonathon's bourbon clinked as he swirled the glass and grinned. 'I'd keep a close eye on her. You know better than most, pretty birds sometimes fly away.'

He would have knocked Sturts out for that comment if they'd been anywhere else. Instead he let the lesser man melt back into crowd.

He wouldn't make any apologies for feeling protective of Serena, and he hadn't been concerned that he could do it. But Sturts was making inquiries about Serena's professional skills now and that worried him.

Sturts owned companies overseas and it wouldn't be beneath him to poach her.

He found Serena locked in conversation with Rachel Bragg. Rachel, taller of the two, stooped over Serena with her usual pretentious air. What concerned David was the way a spindly digit struck out every few moments to stab a hole through Serena's violated personal space. Serena held her ground, neither nodding nor backing away. But David knew body language. Serena was being railroaded by the Queen of Quibble, a situation that needed fixing.

Now.

David cleaved a path through the crowd, which had reached capacity levels. He pulled up inches from Rachel and her talons. Mid-sentence, she stopped. Serena's surprised gaze snapped over too.

'Is there a problem?' he asked.

'David, this is between Serena and me.' Rachel's dismissive expression said butt out.

'Is this pow-wow work-related?'

Rachel scoffed. 'Of course. Serena and I don't see each other privately.'

'Then, I assure you—' David stepped closer '—this concerns me.'

Serena squared her shoulders. 'David, I can handle this. Rachel and I should go to another room and talk about it away from the guests.'

Rachel ignored that suggestion and pierced David with a look. 'Serena has been neglecting her other tasks at the agency. I'm simply letting her know that while it's all very well to laud it up over this feather in her cap, she's still a junior and has other duties to perform.'

David's blood simmered. 'Such as?'

Serena spoke up. 'Really? Can't this wait?'

Rachel's bark drowned her out. 'Like help *me*! Since she's been involved in this campaign, I haven't been able to leave the office before six. I've had to answer my own phone, look after my own correspondence. As for the mail—' She gave a put-upon sigh, and her eyes shot to the ceiling.

David studied Serena's pale face and his ears began to steam. He eyeballed Rachel again. 'This has gone on for weeks and you've said nothing to Serena?'

'Of course I've spoken to her,' she said. 'Several times without result. The other day I'd asked Reception to have my calls redirected. When I came back from lunch, she was out of the office—*again*—and my phone was going berserk. I decided now was the time to be direct.'

'At this launch, here, tonight?' He shot a glance around the packed room. 'In my house with hundreds of guests?'

Rachel blinked, then gave an awkward shrug. 'Perhaps now is a less than appropriate time.' She couldn't keep it at that. 'But it had to be said.'

David turned to Serena. 'Is this true? You haven't kept up with your other duties?'

'Between Jezz and appointments and shoots...' Serena's excuse trailed off.

David redirected his attention to Rachel. 'We've known each other quite a while.' Rachel conceded the point. 'In all that time, though I've wanted to, I've never let you know exactly how I've felt.' Rachel features sharpened. 'Let me start with pretentious, calculating and self-serving. Add annoying, and that pretty well sums up my opinion of you.'

Rachel's dark eyes flashed. 'How dare you talk to me that way? I take very good care of some of your most valued clients.'

'And one other thing. You're fired.'

Rachel shook with anger. *'You can't do that!'*

'Just did. I'll have your belongings forwarded on to your personal address. Any queries, speak to my lawyers.' He'd let them sort it out. Whatever it cost, this was worth it.

David folded Serena's arm in his and led her away. When Rachel was out of sight, he pulled up, looked into Serena's startled eyes and smiled. Then he chuckled.

A heartbeat later, Serena covered her grin with a hand. 'Oh, my.'

David sucked back air and nodded. His feelings for Serena had played a role, but his decision just now was completely justified. 'That woman's had it coming. But you should have told me. I could have done something sooner.'

'I was worried it would cause a problem, and it has. What about her clients?'

'If they decide to follow her, it'll hurt, but we'll survive. But let's forget about that.' He glanced around, then shuffled Serena back into a dark crook. He kissed her till his ears rang and their feet no longer touched the ground.

When he came up for air, her eyes were dreamy, and his loins were anything but. Her back was to a wall. He braced one arm up over her head. The other palm flattened out at her side. Pinned in.

'I need to tell you,' he murmured, 'how delicious you look in that gown.' He hoped that his eyes told her she was even more delicious out of it.

'I'm glad you approve because it cost you a fortune.'

He chuckled. 'Is that what you wanted to tell me earlier? That you used company expenses for your own wicked gain?'

'Not mine. I went to all this trouble for you.'

His raised arm came down and that middle finger scooped around her bodice. He looked into her cleavage. 'How much trouble to take it off?'

She craned a look over his shoulder. He moved to block it. She searched his eyes, then straightened his collar. When her touch curled just below his throat, he leant into it. He should lose the tie more often.

'You're forgetting,' she said, 'we have guests.'

He nudged a little closer. 'I think we should tell everyone that the party's over and it's time for bed.'

He nipped the side of her neck. Mmm, what was that scent? Musk? Floral? All he knew was it did weird and wonderful things to his sensory cells—in fact, all of his working parts.

She dodged and got away, sweeping around him.

He frowned and reached for her hand. 'Hey, get back here.'

Dodging again, she collected her dress's short train and

began to slowly back out. 'The auction's due to start in ten minutes. Clients. Sponsors.' Her crooked finger beckoned him. 'Important campaign, remember?'

He moved out, into the light and…

Of course he remembered.

God, had he ever thought her maturity was an issue? Right now, she was the one taking the lead and focusing on what needed to be done, even if he'd rather be doing something way different.

He started off towards the festivities and the main room with Serena right beside him. 'Okay, let's do this thing.' He arched a brow. 'You ready?'

Her voice was stronger than he'd ever heard it. 'You bet I am.'

CHAPTER TEN

SERENA needed to find David.

At five past midnight, she'd said farewell to the last of her guests. Now she was ready for another brand of party.

She turned a tight circle in the centre of the enormous room, empty but for herself and a few cleaning staff. After hours of noise and excitement, this echoing quiet felt odd. She ran an eye over the quaver balloons hovering high above on the ceiling, then the litter of crystal glasses and finger-food plates strewn over the tables, floor—even the grand piano.

She frowned. Maybe David was outside in the fresh air. She could sure use some.

The air was cool and everything hushed when she slipped out through a set of doors onto a sea of terracotta. An opulent stone fountain held court on the terrace and Serena grinned at its centrepiece—an oversized cherub holding a harp. This estate was certainly magnificent, and a little over-the-top for her tastes. But these surrounds had helped bear out the fairy tale she'd lived tonight.

Her feelings for David had gone past anything she'd ever imagined. Now that she'd spent quality time in his arms, it was difficult to hold on to a concept of how it had been before. There'd been teasing, like now, but back then it had been as boss and employee, or student and mentor. Their relationship had initially been one of opposites in practically every way.

Then he'd given her the opportunity to grow by awarding her the promotion and accepting the 'booth' challenge. Today he'd made love to her with more enthusiasm, truth and depth than she'd thought possible for any man to share with a woman. Just over a month had passed since he'd given her that first gift of faith. Now, for the first time in her life, she was fast approaching the point where she felt truly validated.

Over these weeks she'd taken a huge step, the *right* step, towards becoming the person she believed she could be. But the future didn't end here, tonight. The question she wanted answered was…did her future include David?

A twinkling view of far-off city lights called her. After plucking a bougainvillea bloom from its lattice wall, she twirled the scarlet petals between her fingers and crossed to the terrace's sculptured stone rail.

David appeared to be most everything she'd hoped to find in a man. He certainly fulfilled the requirement on her wish list about making her want him all the time. He was talented *and* insatiable.

She clutched the bloom to her breast.

But did he want to be anyone's long-term Prince Charming? More importantly, did *she* want that attachment? Now, tomorrow and next week were easy. What about next year? Or the year after? She had a goal, and if she sacrificed it now to stay in a relationship…

What if that relationship ended and, along the way, precious opportunities were lost? If she put her dreams on hold, she might discover that she couldn't so easily resurrect them.

Her mother had found that out. She'd won a gold medal in archery, but put competing aside when she'd met Serena's father. Her dad used to make a big deal about what a good cook his wife was, and how nice she kept the house, maybe to make up for it the best way he knew how. He'd always seemed so easygoing back then, before her mum had passed away. But the situation between her and David was different.

Serena dropped the flower over the rail, set her elbows on the ledge and cupped her sensible chin in her level-headed hands.

If they continued seeing each other, how would she know for certain that his work-related compliments were sincere? She didn't want to be patronized. What if, over time, he came to believe that her decisions ought to reflect his own? She wanted to grow, not be stifled.

She straightened.

Perhaps instead of relationships she should stay constant, think about long term, rather than short. About what was best for her, for her future, rather than—

'What are you doing out here alone?'

She whirled around at the deep voice behind her. She wasn't surprised to find David standing there, so tall and broad, a veritable tower. He looked so sexy in his black shirt and trousers. Had a more desirable male ever lived? Did he have any idea just how deeply he affected her?

She willed her heartbeat to quieten, then brushed back a whisper of hair stirred by the breeze. 'I thought I'd get some air.'

He walked over, swept her up in his arms and twirled her around. She shrieked, laughed, and held on tight.

He put her down and gazed into her eyes. 'One hundred and twenty-five grand in the kitty from the auction. That should well and truly cover the expenses for that idea of yours. Two thousand dollars for a Scotch bottle autographed by a seventies legend. Ten-thousand for a T-shirt from a sixties tour? Tonight was a sensation. *You're* a sensation. And talented.' His eyes caressed hers. 'And beautiful.'

And *he* was melting her heart. Making her love him, damn it. She didn't want that. She wasn't ready for anything like it. She wanted to travel, and David's life was here.

'And now that we've put that puppy to bed,' he pressed his lips to her forehead, 'what say we go too?'

Ten minutes ago she might have raced him to the bedroom, but now...

Serena broke their embrace and moved a few paces away. She found a reason to gaze up at the stars. 'Smells like rain's on the way.'

When he joined her, she turned her back and tried to focus on the silver lights of Sydney, the crickets chirping. Maybe if she tried she could wipe out every other sense— his smell, how his breathing deepened, as it did now, when he had plans of them being together.

She smiled to herself. Block David out? Impossible. Her stomach fluttered at the thought of being close to him.

Strong arms wrapped around her middle. His chin rested on her shoulder, then grazed up her cheek. 'It'll be nice sleeping in tomorrow,' he said, 'with the rain on the roof.' He kissed her ear. 'Want another drink?'

She shook her head. One glass was enough. She still needed full use of her faculties. Another glass might change her mind.

He gave her a squeeze. 'Me neither. Let's go to bed.' His rumbling murmur at her ear made her shiver and want him all the more. But she shouldn't.

Should she?

God, she didn't know what she wanted any more.

Her temple pounded with the beginnings of a headache. She really ought to just go home.

'David, I'm very tired—'

'Poor baby.' He swayed her gently. 'I'll rock you to sleep.'

She broke free of his arms. She needed time to think. To decide what she needed to do. What direction she needed to take.

She looked him squarely in the eye. 'I really think I should go home and sleep in my own bed.'

'Serena.' He stepped forward to slay her with the sexiest lidded gaze in the history of seduction. 'Do I need to remind you that we haven't tried *my* bed yet?'

She thought long and hard. God, it was difficult, but, 'I want mine.'

He considered it. 'All right.' He kissed her cheek and kept close. 'Your place then.'

Could she blame him for not listening? Her body was telling her not to listen, too.

'David, I'm worn out.' Physically. Emotionally. All of a sudden she was ready to crumple.

His smile was crooked. 'Should I consider that a compliment?'

She ignored that. 'These weeks have been full on.' And she'd loved every minute of it. Making decisions. Ensuring things were done right. It had made her ultimate goal seem achievable. She *would* get there.

David's expression deepened. His head angled as he

cupped her chin and searched her eyes. 'You *are* tired.' He brushed his lips over her temple. 'I'll drive you home.'

Oh, God, did he have to touch her like that? It made leaving a thousand times more difficult. She didn't want to think about Monday, when she'd see him next. How would she feel? Would she have changed her mind? Would common sense prevail? Or would she beg him to kiss her again?

'The limo Jezz organized is still out front,' she let him know. 'I'll take that. We'll talk Monday.'

She tried to move away, but he held her, then curled that stray wisp behind her ear. His worried gaze probed hers. 'You sure you're all right?'

'I'm *fine*,' she lied. 'I just need some *me* time.' She forced a smile. 'You know how us girls are.'

His expression said he didn't have a clue.

'Serena, I want you to know that today meant a lot to me.'

He was sincere, she was certain. Could she be any less honest? 'It meant a lot to me, too.'

He seemed pleased with that. 'I'll walk you to the car.' She should decline, but another few moments in David's company weren't that easy to resist.

As they moved off he took her hand and lightly swung it. 'And on Monday…'

She waited. 'Yes? What about Monday?'

He tipped sideways towards her. 'You'll have to wait and see.'

CHAPTER ELEVEN

'WHERE the hell *is* she?'

David stood in the doorway of Serena's office, arms bracing the jambs, brain going round in circles, then in reverse. Monday morning. Ten past eleven. Usually she was in by eight.

He shot a look over one shoulder. Mandy Rogers from Accounts stopped her journey and blinked. 'Do you want something, Mr Miles?'

'Where's Serena?' His gaze scanned the room as he strode towards her. Memories of the weekend infused his mind, but he concentrated and set his jaw against the sting in his gut. 'Has she come in yet?'

He'd already gone through the cafeteria, Administration, every department, even the mailroom. The excuse she'd used Saturday night—she was tired, wanted to go home—echoed in his head and that sting in his gut pinched again.

Face tipped up, Mandy gaped at him with eyes wide as dinner plates. 'I haven't seen her yet.' She raised a finger and pointed. 'Maybe someone in Data might know.'

No, he'd been there. Twice.

He shovelled a hand through his hair, and again.

Maybe he should just wait in his office. But these questions and doubts whirling through his brain…

He stopped his raised hand before it ploughed through his hair a third time.

He was overreacting. He wouldn't jump to conclusions. He had faith in Serena. What they'd shared on Saturday wasn't something anyone would enjoy then just toss away. It wasn't the same as their night in the booth. That had been wonderful, but this had been more. They'd moved on from impulse. Taken that next step.

He concentrated on putting one foot in front of the other, on getting back to his office.

And what about her work commitments? Leaving him in the lurch would be the last thing she'd do. He depended on her to keep this campaign on track. Depended on her to keep it all afloat till Jezz was back in full swing. And while it didn't sit well with him to depend on anyone as much as he depended on Serena right now, he could trust her integrity. Just because she was younger than him didn't mean she didn't have standards.

His clenched fist swung sideway and slammed the wall.

If Sturts had gone behind his back, he'd cream the bastard.

Pint-sized Mary Charters tried to trot by. He blocked her and she staggered back, freckled face alarmed.

'Serena Stevens.' He made himself breathe. 'Know where she is?'

'Sorry, Mr Miles. I never go to that side of the building.'

When he nodded, she scurried away.

He needed to sit down with a big steaming cup of black coffee. Tilda could make it extra strong. He'd immerse himself in the Squeezy Orange Juice campaign and, before he knew it, Serena would come bouncing through his door with a good reason why she hadn't answered either her home or cell phone yesterday or this morning.

He trudged into his office.

She couldn't have forgotten their unbelievable afternoon. How she'd soaped up his back and he'd lathered her legs. That first time, when she'd cried out, would remain etched in his memory for ever. Water slipping over limbs, simple touches working miracles...

His chest tightened.

Maybe she'd had an accident.

Tilda looked up from her keyboard. 'Did you find her?'

He pushed in his office door. 'I need the Juice campaign press ideas and coffee.' He saw her owlish expression but couldn't manage a smile. Massaging the knot in his neck, he exhaled and shook his head. 'No, I haven't found her.'

The door swung shut and his intercom buzzed. He forced his feet to move. *Keep busy. Stay focused.* He wouldn't let feelings get a hold of his throat. That was not the way he did things. Not any more. He'd learnt, *damn it.*

The yachts and Opera House shells looked cardboard today. The city surge below antlike, unimportant.

The intercom sounded again. He stared at his desk, uninterested, then depressed the button. 'Tilda, I need that coffee extra strong and now.'

'Mary Charters just rang,' Tilda told him. 'She saw Serena heading towards the paintbox department.'

Immediate streams of relief doused the pain. David fell against his desk and almost laughed. She was here. In this building. Of course she was!

Out the door, he blew Tilda a kiss. 'Don't worry about that coffee. Don't worry about Squeezy Juice. Or any calls. I'm unavailable.'

After the launch, out on the terrace, it had been all he could do not to sling Serena over his shoulder, carry her upstairs and rip that honey of a dress straight off her body. Throughout the auction, he'd grinned in anticipation of her linking her arms around his neck again, of reinventing their earlier adventures, adding some new stuff—there was still so much to learn.

At the time, the pool house had been incredibly satisfying. In fact, the sense of fulfilment had almost frightened him. His mind had whispered about work, the launch, what should be most important. But all bells had been drowned, like pebbles in a rapid, by passion and driving need.

Was Serena the one?

He rounded the last corner, a horse on the home stretch.

He'd get an explanation, make it clear that he'd been worried. She'd soothe him, they'd laugh.

Then he'd give her his surprise.

'*Serena.*'

She glanced up from the artwork she and Dot Booney were working on and almost gasped. David's voice was unmistakable, but she hadn't braced herself for the striking vision that filled the doorway. Black trousers, crisp white shirt, no tie, and eyes stormy enough to stop her heart from beating.

She couldn't tell—was passion the cause of such intensity, or was she in deep trouble?

She set down her pen and looped some hair behind her ear. No use believing she could put off the inevitable. She had to face this some time. Better to get it over and done with.

'Hello, David.'

Dot shuffled aside as David crossed the distance separating them. His eyes burned into hers as a smile cut across his face. 'Where have you been? You worried the hell out of me.'

'I had an appointment downtown.'

The smile flinched. 'And you didn't bother to tell anyone?'

She swallowed the lump that had swollen in her throat and moved to the copying machine in the corner. 'I wanted to get an errand out of the way early. I thought I'd be back by nine.' She collected a pile of quarto sketches, faced him and arched her brow. 'Should I have checked it with you first?'

David kept his gaze on Serena. 'Dot?' The older woman jumped from her startled state. 'Would you excuse us for a moment?' Dot and her size-twenty red overalls bolted from the room. As the door swung half closed behind her David's chin lifted and his broad shoulders rolled back. 'That explains this morning. What about yesterday?'

She coughed out a laugh. 'Would you like a copy of my personal itinerary from now on?' Sleeping together didn't give him the right to know where she was every minute of the day. *Or* think that he should decide for her.

His brows nudged together and face set more. 'You didn't answer your phone.'

Avoiding his eyes, she took a seat behind the desk. 'I turned it off.'

'Didn't you think I might want to speak with you?'

She bit down against a pang of guilt. Yes, she'd known he'd want to speak to her. See her. Hold her. That was why she'd made herself unavailable.

Needing something to occupy her hands, she collected a pencil and pretended to correct a magazine layout. 'I visited my father. I only decided early Sunday.'

Settling down to work in her apartment had been out of the question and Carly had been busy training at her karate dojo. She always called her dad on his birthday; despite his 'father knows best' routine, they still loved each other. Besides, being surrounded by memories of her mother—being in her family home—helped whenever she felt uncertain or upset.

'And you stayed there all night?'

Her gaze flew at him. *Was that an accusation*? 'And if I did?'

He raised his shoulders and opened up his palms. 'Didn't you think about me?'

She'd tried not to think at all! Confused, torn down the middle. How easy would it be to fall into a full-blown relationship? *Too* easy.

She adored David's company, his wit, the way he made her feel so special and unique. If only she'd been any other girl with any other dream. But she didn't want a partner. She wanted to go on with her life the way she'd planned. How could she do that if they continued seeing each other behind the scenes? If she fell in love, her choices would disappear.

She dropped the pencil.

But he was right. She shouldn't have cut him off yesterday. And, to be honest, some part of her delighted at his concern. What if he hadn't tried to contact her till later today? Or tomorrow? What would that have done to her self-esteem?

She exhaled. 'Well, I'm here now.' And calmer, thank heavens. 'What did you want to see me about?'

He moved towards her. 'When we left the terrace, I said you'd have to wait till Monday? You don't remember?'

Those words? How he'd swung her through the air? The way his mouth had pressed and murmured against her brow?

She nodded. 'I remember.'

He frowned over a crooked grin. 'I thought you might be curious.'

Of course she was. She'd tried not to think about his tease. Did he want to give her a bonus? Given their weekend, she'd find that an insult. Or possibly he had in mind something more personal.

During their hours in the pool house he'd whispered how he loved her enthusiasm. Well, maybe it was time she reined back. She didn't want gifts, if that was what this was about. She wanted his respect as a colleague.

When she didn't answer, he moved to hook a hip over a desk corner and tip towards her. 'Would you like to guess?'

Her skin flashed hot.

Guess? She had work to do, schedules to meet. The work she was trying to get done was important to him, too.

She leant back in her chair. 'I really don't have time right now.' It was true. 'I have those proposals—' she clutched a handful of paper '—and this artwork—'

He snatched her hand as it waved by. 'Why are you acting this way?'

She wrenched her hand away. Too much contact. Too much strength and heat.

He followed when she pushed out her chair and moved to the front of the desk.

'What's going on, Serena?' His voice was low, close to dangerous. 'Is there something I should know? From the beginning I said no misunderstandings. Whatever's on your mind, spit it out.'

She clasped her trembling hands together. No more avoiding the issue.

Looking up from her shoes, she met his eyes. 'I really enjoyed our time together in the pool house…'

He spat out a laugh. 'What are you talking about, "enjoyed our time"?' He reached to pull her close. His palm ironed up her arm as his breath warmed her hair. 'You were out of your skin.'

Oh, God, don't do this. She tried breaking free, but he held her firm. He was stronger, in so many ways. She needed a different tack. 'Yes, it was good. Great, in fact. But—'

The pad of his thumb pressed against her lips. 'Try *incredible.*'

When her stomach contracted around a pulse, she weaved around and escaped his hold.

She pulled down a breath. 'I've given it a lot of thought. And this...' she struggled for words '...this relationship we've developed away from the office... I don't know that it will work.'

A shadow moved behind his eyes. 'You don't think so, huh?'

'We should be focusing on this campaign.'

He blinked, then smiled. 'So, you're still committed to that?'

What a question. 'Of course. I said I'd give you my all. I've never meant anything more.'

Her gaze slid to his mouth, how he chewed his lip, as if remembering how she tasted. He crossed his arms. 'And you think sleeping with the boss will interfere with your performance?'

The room shrank as he edged closer.

Needing more space, she stepped back until she hit the desk. 'I'm afraid it will, yes.'

Not only her performance here but also her bigger-picture plans. Sleeping with David threatened the carrot she'd dangled all those years to make it through the marketing assignments, the part-time waitress jobs, her doubts that she would evolve from 'podgy' and 'not so bright' to who she knew she could be if she sacrificed and tried hard enough.

Now she had to sacrifice again. This longing. His heat. Her heart. She could do it. She *must*.

'We have this campaign to finish,' she said. 'To let our feelings get in the way…' She shook her head. 'It won't work.'

When he stepped closer, she wanted to run. 'You've made up your mind?'

Desire curled in her stomach. 'I have.'

'Then I'll have to change it.'

Arms made of iron swept her up off her feet. A belt of adrenaline left her dizzy. Surrender, hovering over her, threatened to fall. 'What are you doing?'

Striding from the room, he kicked the door open the rest of the way. 'I'm taking you home.'

She bobbed against his chest as he marched her down the corridor. She didn't want to lean in against him. That would give the wrong impression. She didn't want that. Didn't want this. Didn't want *him*?

For one blessed moment she let herself enjoy the uncompromising strength surrounding her before offering her remaining excuse. 'I have an appointment in an hour.'

His grin stripped the clothes from her body. 'In an hour you'll be in my bed.'

CHAPTER TWELVE

So it began. Her affair with the boss.

Serena tapped her foot.

Or, so he'd like to think.

In the passenger side of David's Mercedes, which man-oeuvred through the mid-town traffic, she crossed her arms and tried again.

'Just so you know, I'm still not happy about this.'

David slanted a glance and his lip curled into a grin. 'You will be.'

Her toe kept tapping. 'I have meetings this afternoon. Don't you?'

'Uh-huh.'

'Then why can't we discuss this later?' She'd give an inch. 'Tonight if you want.'

That would give her more time to think. Being swept away like a damsel by her knight was pretty hard to resist. When he'd carried her through the building, not caring who saw, she'd insisted he put her down at the lift. He hadn't listened. He still wasn't.

'Hel-lo?' He didn't answer her. 'David? What do you think?'

'Hmm?' He indicated left and swung the wheel. 'Think about what?'

'About discussing this later.'

His smile bespoke indulgence. 'Serena, there's nothing to discuss.'

'Don't I get any say in this?'

His eyes left the road, caressed her throat, then met her gaze. He turned back to the road. 'No.'

Did he think he was a law unto himself? She tugged on her seat belt. 'This is kidnapping.'

'If you want to report me, I'll drop you off.' As the sign of the local police station approached he slowed the car. The truck behind blared its horn. David ignored the warning and finished braking. At a dead stop, he leant over to push her door open. His arm rode over her breasts. The burst of tingles flared right down to her toes.

She battled the rush of arousal, then glared at him. 'You did that on purpose.'

He ducked his head to gain a better view of the police sign. 'There's your stop.' His arm lowered, then dragged over the tops of her legs. He sat up straight while she shivered and fought flash fires. 'Last call.'

The truck blared again. Jumping, she glanced around at the mounting traffic, then flipped her hand at the steering wheel. 'For God's sake, you'll cause an accident.'

'I won't have it said that I forced a lady against her will.'

Three air-horn blasts shook the car. Serena swivelled around. A ten-ton trucky waved his fist from his semi's cabin. She guessed what he was yelling.

She dived back around and pushed David's shoulder. 'Just get moving!'

They didn't talk the rest of the way. By the time the car

cruised up his cobblestone drive, Serena nerves were frazzled. Although she couldn't predict a blow by blow, she knew what he planned…only all the scintillating delights they'd experienced together before.

She couldn't guess where he wanted to complete this seduction…the library, the kitchen, perhaps in a Jacuzzi. Any location would serve. They could make love in a cage, the wonder and thrill would still be amazing.

He cut the engine and pushed on his door. Hugging herself, Serena shivered.

If she let him touch her, let him peel the clothes off her body and worship it as he'd done before, she'd be a goner. Everything she'd kept to the fore of her mind these past years would be put on hold…but for how long?

For ever? Until he got sick of her?

Neither answer was acceptable. She wasn't beaten yet.

The scent of jasmine from a nearby garden bed greeted her as she filled her lungs with courage, then alighted. Her hand in his, they walked up the stairs to the front door. Gilbert appeared before they reached the mat.

In a Hawaiian shirt and cream chinos today, he didn't appear at all surprised to see them.

'Good morning, Miss Stevens.'

What could she say? 'Morning, Gilbert.'

He spoke to David. 'Anything for you, sir?'

'Not today, thanks, Gil.'

'Then I'll be off. I'll see you tomorrow, sir.'

Her skin shrank. She turned on David. 'You teed this up with your house staff?' How embarrassing!

'It was your surprise, no one else's.'

Surprise. 'The afternoon off with you?'

'Something like that.' He grinned and walked in ahead.

She followed and hauled him back. 'David, we have to talk. This—what we're doing—is far too important not to discuss.'

David was exceptional in every way, but Serena knew that, for him, this was about testosterone, the chase, sex, as much as anything. What did *he* have to lose if it didn't work out? If it turned ugly, he'd just hire someone to replace her, as he'd replaced Rachel. Little Miss Stevens would hardly be indispensable after Jezz came back.

But whether this affair lasted a week, a month or a lifetime, it meant the same to her. She would fall in love.

A broken heart delivered courtesy of David Miles might cripple her as badly as giving up the part of her that needed to discover the world. Truly find herself.

He stood before her, his eyes searching hers. Concern gradually creased his brow.

Heartbeat tripping, breathing shallow, she couldn't find the right words. She pressed her lips together. Couldn't he see?

The back of his hand touched the burn of her cheek then a wave of emotion washed over his face. He blinked twice, his eyes squeezed shut and he shook his head, tight and quick, as if chasing away a bad thought.

When his eyes opened they were clouded with doubt. 'God…I thought you wanted this. I thought when I got you here…' His jaw jutted and he stepped away. 'Obviously I was mistaken. I'll take you back to the office.' He walked around her as if she were suddenly contagious.

A sinking feeling rushed through her body. She had to explain. 'David, it's not that simple.'

He wheeled back around. 'Damn it, Serena, what are you afraid of?'

His tone wasn't harsh as much as pleading. She huffed

out a short laugh. What was she afraid of? What the hell? Why not give it up?

'Failure.'

He shrugged. 'Me too.' He came forward and searched out her hand. 'How about trusting me? Let yourself go. Let's see where this takes us.'

She didn't want to take the risk, but she wanted David so much. She'd never deviated from her straight and narrow path like this before. Nothing had been allowed to interfere. And then she'd met him, her boss, her lover. Could she be brave enough to keep following this bend in the road?

The grandfather clock ticked in the corner and David's gaze began to shutter. The grip on her hand eased.

He was giving up? And why wouldn't he? With her being so stubborn and serious and dull, when they could be having fun in this great big house, with its quality artwork, sweeping staircase and lots and lots of rooms...

She released the air from her lungs and kicked his toe with hers. Her mouth curved with a small smile. 'Where this takes us? You know, I've been wondering the whole trip. I had my money on the spa.'

His stern face melted and he drew up to his tallest. 'Which one?' He looked over his shoulder, a mischievous gleam in his eyes as he tugged her along. 'We have three.'

'Oh! Only *three*.'

David was everything she'd dreamed the man in her distant future would be, the entire package and a thousand times more. Yet this was the present, and David was now.

Her palm pressed the knot in her stomach, the one her father would tell her to heed. But her feet found the stairs. She breathed in and began to climb.

David took each step in front of her. Every so often, he'd glance ahead as if to make sure they were on track.

'I thought we'd try something different,' he told her, 'and stay away from water and small spaces.'

She almost laughed but stopped. 'Please don't tell me you've planned something out in the open because I won't join you.'

His finger tinkled her palm. 'Spoilsport.'

She wouldn't take a chance. 'I include balconies and rooftops in out-in-the-open.'

'Can't say I'm not disappointed.'

At the top of the stairs, they turned a corner and Serena swallowed as her heart leapt to her throat. She stepped inside. Well, of course. *'Your bedroom.'*

Moving around to face her, he found both her hands and, walking backwards, guided her into a suite as large as her apartment. Strips of sunshine fell through half-drawn timber shutters onto the—

She shook her head. 'White pile carpet? This just isn't you.'

The bed definitely was. King-sized with bold timber scrolls, top and tail. The duvet wasn't quite gold or caramel or fawn, but its fabric was rich and littered with scatter cushions, crimson, cream and midnight silk blue.

He gathered her in and she remembered all this was real.

'A long time ago, this was a guest room.' As if he couldn't wait another minute, he met her mouth with a penetrating kiss.

When it ended, she roused herself enough to lick her lips. 'Mmm…lucky guests.'

Her gaze fell. The tugging was David's fingers tripping over her blouse buttons.

'Things like carpet,' he said, concentrating, 'aren't important to me.'

In for a penny...

She wrestled his tie apart, then threw it in the air.

'So tell me...' she yanked the tails out from his trousers. '...what *is* important to you?'

'Two things.' They each shrugged the other out of their shirts. 'I won't tell you the first one.'

Was it *her*? Lord, of course not.

She tried not to sound disappointed. 'What's the other?'

His gaze measured her lips. 'You.'

Ripples of want drifted out from her centre as he held her upper arms and drew her near. His thumbs rubbed as his mouth joined hers. The sensation, the deliverance, seemed to set her soul free.

With a contented sound, he broke away, then slid down to his knees. Her red pencil skirt loosened and slipped to her feet before he cupped her hips to bring her in. Heat and longing radiated from every pore when he nuzzled the hollow at one side of her tummy. She felt sick with longing by the time he looked up and grinned. 'No black silk today?'

Her jaw dropped. She'd forgotten. Did she have the courage to check?

Yep. 'White cotton.'

His fingers feathered her sides as he stood again. 'Believe me, you'd be sexy in orange pantaloons.'

Did he mean that? He found her attractive—okay. But would he think morning raccoon eyes were sexy? What if she had a really bad bug? Would he still think she was gorgeous looking like death while he brought her cups of soup for a week?

She couldn't resist. 'What if I put on fifty pounds and wore cola-bottle lenses?'

'What if I lay you on my sheets now and whisper all the things that make you irresistible?'

He whispered at her ear as he gathered her up and laid her on the cool silk. He whispered as he undressed her then stroked her and caressed her. When she lost her ability to speak, he, too, fell quiet, stepped back, kicked off his shoes, then his trousers. He stood before her…David, her David. More perfect than the statue.

He sank in beside her onto a mattress as soft as clouds. His touch curled around her cheek as he nipped her chin and ground into her side. 'Can you guess how many times these past weeks I've dreamt of lying here with you?'

Two fingers walked up her ribs to find then pluck her nipple. Smiling, she wreathed and rolled into him. 'Did you count?' She hadn't.

'A boy doesn't *count* when he dreams of his girl.'

Dreams of his girl.

The pleasure in those words almost bested his palm skating across her breasts, over her stomach, down, down…

When she gasped, he burrowed beneath her hair. 'You smell so good. What perfume do you wear?'

Her hand clapped over his and worked with it. She concentrated on the lights and pulse getting brighter, bigger. Maybe she should answer him. 'It's not Chanel No. 5.'

His teeth tugged her ear. Every nerve-ending in her left side sang while that ache throbbed and grew. She needed to get closer.

Flinging a leg over his hip, she sipped from the hollow at his throat, then brushed her lips down through the granite and hair as he stroked and gently rocked. Why on earth had she thought coming here today was a bad idea?

Their previous times together had been exciting, naughty, something she read about or other people did. This afternoon spoke to her in a different way. Still drugging and delicious, compelling and incomparable. But deeper than that. This time he touched her on a higher level, a level she'd never left exposed. A hidden part. To share with him.

His fevered skin slid and soaked over hers as she flew nearer the edge. Almost there, almost, almost...

His hand slipped away. Every taut muscle let go. Her heartbeat boomed through her veins as she opened her eyes and groaned. But he was moving over her.

Her arms wound around his neck as he positioned himself.

'Missionary position—' he grinned '—on a bed, no less.'

He found her ready. Eyes drifting shut, she rotated her hips and urged him on. 'Too boring for you?'

He began to move. 'What do you think?'

As the stars in her head gathered and friction coiled tight she couldn't think at all. But when they leapt off into star-bursts at the same time, one thought came to mind. It made her the happiest she'd ever been.

As well as the saddest.

CHAPTER THIRTEEN

I NEVER want to let her go.

Lying among the rumpled sheets, resting on an elbow, head cradled in his palm, David gazed over at Serena sitting on the window seat. The blinds, pulled wide, flooded the room with light, making her glow like an angel wearing an oversized white bathrobe. His dog snoozed on the seat beside her, her snout resting on Serena's lap. Sylvie was snoring.

'Give her a prod.' David pushed up and swung his legs over the side of the bed. 'Once she gets that engine going, it's enough to shake the foundations.'

Threading her fingers through Sylvie's coat, Serena raised her chin. 'She's finally decided to come out of her hiding place and say hello. I'm not going to do anything to risk our friendship.'

In her sleep, Sylvie snorted and her back leg kicked out.

David reached out for Serena. 'Leave that dog alone and come back here to me.'

'A woman's work...' She ruffled Sylvie's ear and strolled over, tightening the sash at her waist.

'Don't bother about that. We've showered, rested up,

taken in provisions.' When she sank in beside him, he leant against her till her back met fine Egyptian cotton. He tasted her exposed throat. 'Now it's time for recreation.'

She put on a sigh. 'What? Again?'

When he felt her melt beneath him, he shifted farther up the bed and tugged the sash. 'Isn't this better than rubbing my dog's ears?'

He studied her mouth—parted, welcoming—and lowered his head.

Serena suddenly gasped.

She knocked him out the way and sat bolt upright. His lower lip stung where her forehead had belted him.

'Oh, God. I had a three o'clock with an alderman today. He wanted to discuss an open-air concert. What time is it?' She clutched his arm. 'Two-thirty.' She leapt away. 'Still time.'

Unperturbed, he fell back onto the bed. 'Relax. I asked Tilda to go through your appointment book and cancel everything. You heard me phone her on the drive here.'

'But I'm not sure I pencilled him in. He called late Friday. I was rushed.'

He reassured her. 'I'll call tomorrow and explain.'

'That we had the day off to wrinkle the sheets?' She pulled a pained face. 'How unprofessional.'

His eyes followed her as she collected her clothes still strewn over the floor.

'This is the first time I've had off work in so many years I can't remember. And it's not a whole day. It's an afternoon.'

The robe came off and those cotton briefs worked their way up over her wiggling behind. 'I've *never* had time off work.'

He should be impressed. 'Then it's time you did.'

A cream lace bra covered breasts he'd come to adore.

She clasped the back strap. 'Not when I'm letting people down.'

He joined her and wondered if he should start stripping her again. Not that he felt underdressed. He felt great.

'I own the company, Serena. Believe me, you're not letting me down.' Skirt on and zipped. Frowning, he grabbed her hand. 'Settle down. Let's focus on what's important here.'

She pinned him with a look. 'I wish you would.'

Spitfire. He loved this different side of her.

After hiding his grin by rubbing the corner of his eye, he crossed the room back to the bed. 'Although I know your answer, maybe you want to explain that last comment.'

Her blouse covered cinnamon-tinted skin. Smooth skin. Good to kiss.

'When you promoted me,' she said, probably searching for her shoes now, 'winning the top award for this campaign meant everything. The sponsors indicated they were prepared to take their business elsewhere and they'd take others with them. We had to win gold. Is that right?'

He spread out on his belly, chin on stacked fists. 'That's right.'

She stopped and looked at him hard. 'It's still *my* priority, but is it yours? Because lately you're sure not acting like it.'

He stared at her. Amazing. 'That really is the most important thing to you, isn't it?'

One part of him applauded. Another wanted to remind her of what they'd shared. Not sex—more than bodies grinding and giving into the push. They'd done that, too, and it had been fantastic. But what had today meant to her? His words, her surrender? They meant a huge deal to him.

His grinding teeth echoed in his skull. 'Sorry to make you choose between the alderman and me.'

Her gaze flew up from where she searched under the bed. 'That is the most childish thing I've ever heard.' She dragged out a shoe.

He sat up. Damn it, she was right. This wasn't about her choosing between men.

He patted down the air while she whipped around the room in one heel. This had gone too far. 'Serena, no one's going to sack you. You don't have to choose between your job and me.'

She stopped to stare. 'Why do I get the feeling I'm the only one making sense?'

'It's *one afternoon*, for God's sake. If I didn't think we could spare it, we wouldn't be here now.'

But that wasn't completely true. He'd wanted to confirm *this* with her today, not tomorrow, not tonight. *Today.* Saturday he'd been understanding. Sunday had driven him mad. She'd played her games, but she didn't hold the gavel in this court. 'As far as work's concerned, I set the agenda. All you have to do is follow my directions.'

She blinked several times, as though an idea had just landed, then smoothed down the sides of her skirt. 'Okay, you're the boss. But I'm still a little confused, so answer me this. You're worth more than the guy who invented toothpaste, yes?'

He set his jaw. Who wanted to discuss money? But he'd indulge her. 'Perhaps.'

She strode over. 'If it all went belly up—this campaign, your agency—you could invest in some other business. You could invest in ten. So, really—' she punctuated each word '—what's the big deal?'

The tips of his ears began to burn. He'd thought he'd come to know her. Guess they didn't know each other that well after all.

'Is it so difficult for you to work out? I could write it on a blackboard, if you like.'

Wariness flickered in her eyes. She'd said too much, overstepped the line, and she knew it. 'I'm trying to understand, that's all.'

'Earlier today you said you were afraid of failure.' All ears now, she backed up, lowered herself onto the window seat and massaged Sylvie's sleeping head. 'Some people don't give a damn about that. They care so little they don't try to achieve jackshit. Why do some people care and others not?'

She dropped her eyes, as if she knew, understood, but wouldn't say.

A fire seared the pit of his gut. 'I will do anything to keep the agency, not only alive, but succeeding and achieving, because if I don't, I'll have lost something more valuable than a mansion with three spa baths. I'll lose my name, my face, my pride. Once was enough. Nothing and no one will see me that low again.'

He didn't do sacrifice and he didn't do—

The fire in his belly snuffed out. His body went cold as he stared down at his open palms.

Was this love?

When she joined him on the bed, they sat side by side, both facing the shutters, neither speaking for the longest time.

'David, you don't have to tell me, but…'

'You want the rest of the story? When I made a complete

ass of myself?' Why not? His past wasn't a federal secret. He didn't post Christmas cards about that incident, but neither did he try to hide it.

She shook her head at her lap. 'I didn't call you an ass.'

'No, I did.' He scrubbed his jaw and pushed out a breath. 'Let me give you the short-but-sweet version, and there are a couple of similarities, so don't take offence.'

Serena held herself tight and listened. And she ought to go right on listening. She'd pushed too far. David was in charge with regard to work, just as he'd said. But should this argument be a surprise? When relationships got complicated, so did everything else. This proved it.

David rubbed the back of his neck and began. 'Years ago when I first set up shop, I fell for a woman who seemed like a good idea at the time. She worked for me, I promoted her and, when I needed her most, she skipped town.'

Serena's face went numb. David wasn't looking at her. Why? Because he was seeing this other woman reincarnated? Only she would never up and walk out in the middle of this campaign. That was what this whole argument was about—her wanting to get the job done while David wanted to roll around. 'What did you do?'

'I wanted to throw in the towel. My client base was poor to don't-worry-about-it. I'm sure there were those in the industry who shook their heads and sighed at the young pup who'd played ball in the wrong park. I was *this* close to chucking it in and joining the forces.'

'Army? Navy?'

'Air force.'

Paper planes. Of course.

'I'd always wanted to fly jets,' he went on, 'but when my

father fell ill and my mother couldn't cope, I decided to stay close to home. I have a younger brother. He needed a male role model during his teenage years. They can be tough.'

Tell me about it. She moved a little closer. 'What happened? Did your family situation hold you back again?'

'By then both my parents were gone and my brother lived in London.'

'So, why not fly?'

His shoulders went back. 'Stubbornness. Pride. And maybe a part of me that thought it was too late. That my life had taken another direction, for better or for worse.'

He'd had a dream and let it go? Suddenly she felt a thousand times closer to him and yet further apart. Would he ever expect her to give up her dream, too?

'I still had one decent-sized client,' he said, 'who for some strange reason believed in me. I didn't want to let him down. I brushed myself off and decided the only way I could do it was to make sure I ended up the best. One hell of a motivational tool. Now it's ingrained. I can't fail again. It's not an option.'

'Yet here you are today playing hooky with me?'

He glanced over and grinned. 'Who was the wise woman who once said everyone needs to break free some time or explode. We've worked hard. We deserve a reward.'

An apology hovered on the tip of her tongue. Guess she'd overreacted about that appointment.

She caught the time on his watch.

Too late to make it now.

She pushed to her feet. 'If you don't mind, I'll call Tilda to make sure she cancelled the alderman.'

He grabbed an extension off the side table. 'Let me.'

Two minutes, and it was confirmed.

'See?' He hung up. 'No earthquakes.' He collected her and eased her carefully back down amongst the cushions. 'Now, if you don't mind, I'm going to make the most of a rare afternoon off.'

He drew her leg up over his lap.

Serena had to laugh. 'What on earth are you doing with my toes?'

He stroked each one. 'I'm not sure yet. But I have a feeling we'll both like it.'

CHAPTER FOURTEEN

SERENA yelped at the slap on her behind and spun around.

Luna Park was famous for its laughing face entrance, traditional carousel and giant slides. The park's Coney Island, with its Wonky Walk and Barrels of Fun, was the perfect location for today's publicity shoot, which she'd dubbed 'Hit the Fun Time.' Everyone had their favourite ride. As Serena rubbed her butt and faced David's devilish grin, she got the impression he had plans for the privacy of the ghost train.

David wrapped his arms around her. Tucking her head under his chin, he stroked the spot. 'Here, let me do that.'

She shoved his hand away and tried to sound stern. 'That hurt.'

'You didn't complain last night.'

She smiled to herself and moved towards the Turkey Trot to grab her bag. 'Last night was different. This is work.'

'And you're doing a fabulous job.'

She struck a curious face. 'How would you know? You've only just arrived.'

'I know because everything you do is fabulous.'

Really?

All warm inside, she played it up and sent a droll look over one shoulder as she walked away. 'Everything?'

'You know damn well you do.' He grabbed her hands and pulled her onto the Trot. As she went up he came down and snatched a kiss. 'Let's go somewhere dark and good for cuddling.'

Grinning, she rolled her eyes. 'I knew it. The ghost train.' She left him behind to collect some folders.

His mouth was at her ear. 'I can squeeze your hand and you can squeeze my—'

'*David.*' Trying not to smile, she darted looks around at the crowd, then moved away. 'This is a public place. I'm working.'

He took the folders from her. 'You've finished work for the day. We've barely seen each other all week. It's Friday night and we're spending it together. Leave that stuff there.' He set the folders on a nearby table, snared her hand and led her off. 'William?'

Acting as if he hadn't seen them misbehaving, her young assistant tipped up his blond mop. Assorted equipment from the day's shoot lay at his feet. 'Yes, Mr Miles?'

'Take care of the rest of this, will you? Thanks a lot. See you Monday.'

A thumbs-up and William continued the task.

Resistance was futile. Serena relented and they fell into step. 'That's not fair.'

'What's not?'

'Me, leaving everything for someone else to tidy up.' She'd come from a family where no one was above pitching in. 'Many hands make light work.'

He tapped her nose with his finger. 'It's called delegation—something you must learn to do. You look after the shoot, William looks after the packing, and I look after you.'

She made a face. 'I'm not sure that makes much sense.'

'It makes perfect sense to me.'

Over this last month, David had relaxed more and more. One reason could be that Jezz was well and back on board, although Serena hadn't handed over the reins. Seemed the sponsors were happy with the direction the campaign had taken. They wanted Serena at the helm. David had been so proud. He'd taken her to the best restaurant in Sydney and bought the finest champagne, although she suspected the special treatment was partly to make up for nixing one of her best-loved ideas the day before. Jezz was delighted for her assistant's more permanent promotion, and Serena was happy, too. Another feather in her cap. Another tick for her résumé.

Another reason to stay here?

Outside the Coney Island enclosed complex, the park was in full swing. Tourists munched hot dogs while children squealed on the roller coaster and seagulls wheeled high above. A perfect afternoon.

She stole a glance at David.

Just perfect.

The pole of the 'Hi-Striker' caught her eye and she hauled him over. She read the sign. 'Test your strength. Bet you can't hit the top.'

The ticket collector offered a big rubber mallet, but David shook his head and pulled her away. 'You don't have any control over that. No one hits the top.'

Serena stopped and pegged her arms out like wings. 'Buck, buck-buck-buck, ba-urck.'

He wore a short-sleeved jersey knit today. His biceps bulged beneath the cuffs as he crossed his arms. 'Nope. Nothing you do will change my mind.' That scuffed eyebrow lifted along with one index finger. 'However, I will win you the biggest fluffy toy in the park.'

He strode off and she followed, skipping behind him like someone half her age. 'You're not going to play the Laughing Clowns, are you?'

He stopped and smacked his chest. 'Do I look like someone who would play the laughing clowns?'

She almost giggled. 'No, you don't.'

He rolled his eyes. 'That's a relief.'

He held her hand as they walked over to a stall. When he handed over a coupon, a portly man with a big smile allocated five darts.

'This is my kinda game.' He surveyed the back wall, which was decorated with scores of inflated balloons. He squeezed one eye closed and took aim. 'Red balloon, left corner.' The dart flew from his hand and—*pop*! 'Blue balloon, second from top right.' *Pop*!

Eighteen more consecutive pops, and he won a gigantic pink koala.

Serena's heart felt almost too full when he handed the prize over. She buried her chin in between its ears. 'I always wanted someone to do that for me.'

'And I *never* wanted to.' He bent so his eyes were level with hers. 'Until you.'

He was about to kiss her when a different light filled his eyes. He drew up tall and peered over her head. 'Want to try the Ferris wheel?'

She looked across as the coloured lights decorating the spokes blinked on for the night.

He took her hand again. 'I haven't been on one of those since I was a kid.'

Heights weren't Serena's biggest strength—nothing

chronic, as her homesickness had once been. But she'd be okay if she didn't look down.

'Sure.' She smiled. 'It'll be fun.'

'*Then* we visit the ghost train.'

'Then the dodgem cars.'

He winked. 'I knew I liked you.'

David handed the ticket collector two coupons and Serena stepped up into the sparkly red carriage. The carriage swung when he plonked the pink bear in the opposite seat then sat beside her. As the wheel began to turn he gathered her in. His mouth dropped over hers and they floated off together, becoming part of the carnival's motion and music.

His eyes were smouldering when he drew away. 'You keep tasting better and better.'

'That's fairy floss.'

His tongue tickled the side of her mouth and she laughed. 'Mmm. Didn't know I had a sweet tooth.' Holding both her hands in his lap, he leant back. 'Are you hungry for more than cotton candy?'

'Are you talking about food or you?'

He pretended offence. 'Both, of course. There's a new Thai place down the road from home. We could get a corner table with a glowing candle, or order take-out and feed each other noodles in bed.'

'Decisions, decisions.' Tapping her chin, she pretended to decide. 'Noodle swapping, I think.'

The distant roar of a jet's engine faded in. They both gazed up as the wheel went round.

David murmured, 'Wonder what it's like to pilot one of those?'

Over these weeks, she'd come to know David better.

Reading the Sunday paper in the sun made him happy. Traffic jams made him angry. He hadn't told her yet what made him sad. She was slowly piecing together the man David was and how he'd got there.

'If flying was such a passion—' she snuggled into him, '—why didn't you take lessons growing up?' Money wouldn't have been a problem.

When she was ten, she'd wanted a horse to ride in gymkhanas—she still thought horses were the noblest creatures on earth—but her dad had said the cost was too high. Every week for two years he'd taken her to the local horse-riding club though, which had pretty much made up for it.

David's thumb brushed back and forth over the top of her hand. 'I would have done anything for that, but my mother was paranoid about most things. Microwave cooking. Greenhouse effect. Whether my shoes were clean. She refused to discuss flying, and my father wouldn't go against her where we boys were concerned. So, I resigned myself to the fact that I'd wait till I was eighteen and old enough not to ask permission.'

'Then your dad got sick?'

He nodded. 'And my hands were full. Besides, I didn't want to add to my mother's upset.'

Serena stretched up and pressed her lips to his sandpaper cheek. 'They were lucky to have a son like you.'

He shrugged it off. 'Any half-decent person would have done the same. You have a responsibility to those you love. You don't set out to hurt their feelings or up and leave when you're needed, do you?'

Serena's soul shrank in upon itself. That was a rhetorical question. He wasn't asking if she would ever disrespect his feelings or needs. Wasn't asking if she would ever leave him…was he?

How could she answer that? She didn't want to hurt anyone. He'd been the one to chase, telling her to trust him and see where their attraction went. Now she knew. A place where she'd never been more certain or more confused.

She loved David. Once she'd walked up the staircase to his bedroom, love had been inevitable. One part of her wanted to spend her life with him, but she couldn't give up that other part of herself. She wanted to stay *and* she wanted to go. She wanted to celebrate how she felt about him, not grow to resent it.

'I see you received flowers.'

She'd been gazing at the last of the afternoon sun-sparkles flashing across the harbour waters.

She frowned. 'Flowers?' Then it clicked. 'You mean the white roses.'

David sent her bouquets filled with colour—bright yellows, vibrant purples, always with the same message: 'Tonight?'

'Who are they from?' he asked.

David would have seen them on her desk. She hadn't taken them home. They were business-related, not personal.

'Jonathon Sturts had them delivered this morning.'

David's chin kicked up as he looked over the edge down at the ground too many metres below. He tugged his ear. 'Why did Sturts send you flowers?'

'A congratulations on the billboards that went up yesterday. He said they were some of the best he'd seen.'

'Does he speak to you often?'

'Every week or so. He says he's taken a personal interest in this campaign.'

'More like a personal interest in you.'

Serena stopped. She rocked forward and a laugh escaped. 'My God, are you *jealous*?'

His face was as dark as his eyes. 'I'm concerned.'

'Why?' She was both flattered and shocked. 'Because another professional is interested in my work?'

'That's exactly why. Be careful of Sturts. He's a charmer.'

'I'm not the least bit interested. How could I be when I have you?'

But for how long? Her mind couldn't skip around the question. In time, would he tire of her? Apparently he hadn't done long-term since Olivia.

When she and David were together, he acted as though he was in love with her, but he hadn't said those three little words—the words she both longed and dreaded to hear. Maybe this was a fling for David. Maybe the most she'd have to decide was what to wear on the plane after he dropped her.

'I'm not talking about attraction, Serena. I'm talking about Sturts tempting you…' His voice trailed off.

'With flowers? I'm not *that* easy. Well, only for you.' She smiled and while she thought he was trying, the humour had gone from his eyes.

They went round twice more. She cuddled into his arm and every so often he kissed her brow.

As the wheel arced to the top again he sat up, holding her shoulders as he faced her. His look penetrated her heart.

'You do wicked things to me, Serena.' He brought her close and slanted his face against hers, their noses side by side, his mouth brushing hers. His arms were strength and shelter, his chest all comfort and steel. 'You make me feel like Samson.' He stole a kiss. 'So strong and so damn…'

He kissed her deeply and she dissolved beneath his need. He filled her up with every kind of wonder. Made her glow and blossom in ways most people would never know.

She did wicked things to him? He did dreadful things to her. She wanted him to keep doing them and for this ride to never end.

CHAPTER FIFTEEN

JEZZ glanced up from her desk and smiled. 'What are you doing in here? Didn't anyone tell you it's Sunday?'

'Says who? Miss Work-Around-the-Clock?' Serena grinned and headed for the guest chair. 'David needed to come in. I thought we'd grab the papers and spread out a picnic blanket in the park for a couple of hours afterwards.'

Jezz's gaze lowered back to the computer-generated sketch she'd been checking. 'You two have gotten real close.'

Halfway down in her seat, Serena paused and stood back up. Was that a negative note in Jezz's voice?

'You were the first person I confided in.' Not that David seemed overly concerned about keeping their relationship outside work a secret. 'I thought you were happy about it.'

Shoulders dropping, Jezz pushed the sketch aside. 'Oh, honey, I am. You and David go together like pancakes and syrup. It's just…' Her gaze wavered, then slipped again.

Serena's stomach tightened. This wasn't like Jezz. She was forthright, always open. What was she avoiding?

'Has something happened? Is it David?' These days her and Jezz's relationship was more like mother and daughter. Mothers looked out for their children, had a way of knowing things that might cause pain or heartache.

Serena's stomach churned. She reached for the heart around her neck, remembered she'd left it on David's bathroom counter, and rounded the desk. 'Tell me what's wrong.'

Jezz slowly stood. 'I got a phone call from Jon Sturts Friday. You know we've been in touch a bit because of my music background. Anyway, he asked about you.'

'Jonathon?' Serena's mind stumbled back. 'Why didn't he phone me himself? What did he want?'

Jezz blinked a few times. 'Serena, he wants *you*.'

Those words…they didn't make sense, not in that context. There was some mistake, a misunderstanding. 'Jonathon wants me? Wants me for *what*?'

She thought of the flowers. David's words…'he's a charmer'…and a hot prickling flashed over her skin.

She backed up. 'But I've never given him any indication I was interested. I'm not. Could never be…'

'He doesn't want you *that* way.' Jezz reached for Serena's arm. 'Jonathon asked about your performance here. Whether you were as good as he believed. Of course, I said you were better than brilliant. Only need to read the papers and talk to your clients to know that. We'll have that award David needs, nothing surer.'

So, that was where this was headed. 'Jonathon wants me to *work* for him?' Jezz nodded. Serena let loose a laugh. 'But I can't. I wouldn't. I love what I'm doing here. David still needs me. I can't leave.'

Her heartbeat hitched. Was that true? Was that her final decision? If he wanted her here indefinitely, she would forgo the idea of working overseas? How could they ever reach a compromise? A long-distance affair? But that wouldn't satisfy either of them.

At one point she'd decided David was so wealthy, he could hire a manager to supervise the agency. But, while that might work for a vacation, a man like David Miles wouldn't hang off someone's coattails, no matter who it was. He'd want his previous life back and be where he wanted to be, do what he wanted to do. Her heart broke to acknowledge that, but it was true, and she couldn't blame him. She felt the same way.

Jezz returned to her seat. 'Jon Sturts is a beat away from sacking his person in London. He needs a replacement. Someone with tenacity, intelligence and sparkle. It's the top job. No supervision. Mayfair apartment provided. He wanted me to run it by you first. Try to convince you. He told me the salary figure, I'm sure just to boast. It's a small fortune.'

Serena shook her head, but her mind was still frozen. 'David gave me this chance. He believes in me.'

Yes, he'd knocked back another of her ideas recently, one she'd had high hopes for. But she hadn't been convincing enough, that was all.

Her head began to swim.

Then last Thursday he'd pulled the plug on a national radio interview. He'd said it was bad timing. She still believed it had been spot on. He'd held her hand and told her not to be disappointed—she was still the best account exec he'd known. He meant it. He must. She was good at this, really good at something, finally.

So, why in her heart did she feel as if he'd begun to hold her back?

Jezz sat forward. 'Jon said if you were interested, he'd slot you in, pronto. That the better man will have won and David would cope.'

Better man? My God. 'What did you say to that?'

'If he wants to keep his baritone, best not to run into David anytime soon.'

'Someone mention my name?'

Serena jumped at the sound of that deep voice. She spun around and he was there, smiling and striding up to her. '*David*.' She patted the moisture broken on her hairline. 'You scared the daylights out of me.'

'You're *white*.' He frowned and brushed the hair from her cheek as he joined her. 'Are you ill? I think you should lie down.'

Maybe she should. Maybe she should hide under the covers and block her ears. She didn't want to be around when David found out about this. She didn't want to listen to those whispers about being held back.

Sounding overly chirpy, Jezz spoke up. 'Serena thought reading papers in the park sounded like a nice way to spend Sunday. You kids should get moving before the whole day's gone. Serena, hon—' she sent a meaningful look '—we'll talk later.'

They said goodbye to Jezz, but, walking down the corridor, Serena still felt sick to her stomach. In three months she'd gone from 'junior' to 'in charge' to 'star'. Who would have dreamed it possible? Remarkable and, in so many ways, not what she'd anticipated. She'd wanted to prove herself, and she'd done it. A fantastic position, a full-time man. But now she was faced with the truth.

She'd planned on a *job overseas* and *nothing permanent*. Suddenly she had an opportunity for 'a'; what did she do about 'b'? Had she even left herself a choice?

'Maybe we should go home and rest.' David's arm linked around her waist. 'I can put you to bed and—'

'Make love to me?' That could only make her feel better.

'I was going to suggest aspirin, but the former works better for me personally.'

She moved to loop her arm through his. 'Let's get some fresh air first. We'll grab every newspaper and maybe some warm scones.'

She could agonize over it till her hair turned grey. For now she was here with the man she loved, doing the job she loved almost as much. She would face Jonathon when the time came…decide about the overseas issue when she needed to.

Her heartbeat hiccuped.

Had her mother thought the same about her passion? That eventually she'd get back to competing?

David kissed her hand. 'Hope you're feeling okay by next weekend.'

Serena filed away her negative thoughts. Why not live for now, even for a while? 'What do you have in mind?'

'A romantic trip into the mountains. A secluded resort, a beautiful meal, some music, maybe a cosy fire.'

She laughed. 'A fire in December? We live down-under, remember?'

His mouth hooked to one side. 'Maybe we should do the *tropical island weekend getaway*. How do sultry nights, warm water lapping your ankles and powder-fine beaches sound to you?'

'Fabulous. Which island?'

'Mauritius?'

She gaped. 'Off the coast of *Africa*?' She dug a knuckle into his ribs and he jumped back. 'You're crazy.'

'You're right. We'd need at least a week there and we can't spare the time. The Barrier Reef is the more sensible option.'

'Are you serious?'

'It's so busy around here, and I don't see it easing up. If we don't steal some time, we'll never get it. Besides—' he hooked her arm more securely through his '—I know you'd enjoy getting away from here for a while. See a few places. Experience some new things.'

Serena's heart felt full to bursting. He was thinking of her, knowing she wanted to travel. He couldn't give her exactly what she'd planned. Was he making up for it the best way he knew how?

Maybe they should talk about it. But maybe that would only stir up a pot that was a ways from boiling over yet. Maybe she should just stop thinking and enjoy this time. Forget about plans, or his proposal knock-backs, or mistimed opportunities.

Maybe she should simply think about *them*.

David rubbed his temple as they walked past Accounts. 'I went over that proposal you gave me Friday.'

Serena perked up. She *loved* that idea—an interactive auction on *Hits* leading up to Easter. An event bigger and brighter than anything she'd tried before.

'The auction at the launch gave me the idea,' she said as they moved into her office to collect her bag. 'We could sneak thirty seconds at the front end of commercial breaks. Promote one item at a time and provide a number for bids. The total amount raised would be announced during an Easter special. The media would pick it up without us needing to pay for time or space and the proceeds could go to helping some worthwhile cause like natural disaster relief. It would give the show's profile another unexpected edge and the publicity would be *incredible*.'

With a crooked smile, he stopped and turned to concentrate on her eyes. 'Hey, slow down.' He brought her hands to his chest. 'You're moving too fast.'

Her back stiffened. Too fast? 'It's *time* to move. This show is the most watched programme in the country. Everyone from six to sixty is tuned in. With some more hard work, we could do amazing things.' Brow low, he started walking again. Good. He was listening. 'I'll need to get the best memorabilia. Promote the pants off it. Invite everyone, particularly overseas parties, to bid. We'd need a Web site…'

Serena could have talked for hours about the possibilities, the endless scope. When she'd finished they'd reached her office and his expression hadn't changed.

'That all sounds very nice,' he said.

Was that a patronizing edge to his tone? She moved over to her desk and began sorting out files for tomorrow's early meeting. 'It's not meant to be *nice*, David.'

She swallowed the quiver in her voice. This wasn't the right time. Perhaps she should drop this discussion for now.

But, damn it, she *couldn't*.

The files thumped back down on the timber. 'This event could be phenomenal. This is supposed to make a *difference*.'

'We're *supposed* to make advertisements. You're an account executive, not Mother Teresa.' Expression softening, he offered a sympathetic smile. 'Why don't we leave the world relief to those who do it best?'

She could hardly believe it. She'd spent days on the proposal. 'Is that it? End of discussion?'

His arms wove over his chest. 'I admire your lateral thinking and generous spirit, but this just won't work. Too much, too soon. This campaign is picking up speed. We need to walk before we can fly.'

She shouldn't feel this desperate. Maybe he was right. But, 'It wouldn't be impossible. Just a challenge. How do you know for sure it won't work?'

'Experience, for one thing,' he stated. 'Logic, another.'

An icicle dripped down her spine. 'Are you suggesting I lack good judgment?'

Serena heard herself and knew she should zip it. But, hell, she also knew this idea had real merit. She could *make* it happen. She simply needed some support. The same faith he'd shown her in the beginning.

Kernels of doubt popped and took shape.

The more she succeeded the more he seemed to want to dismiss her ideas.

Trying to blink her agitation down, Serena crossed to the other side of the room. When she turned around, her Go Girl mug seemed to goad her from its coaster on her desk.

She clenched her jaw, found her strength and a diplomatic tone. 'I understand you've been in this game a long time…'

He sent an arch look. 'You make me sound like Methuselah.'

'…But this is my campaign, and with the evidence of public approval to back me up—'

'Whoa. Slow down.' David held up a hand and joined her. 'You've done a terrific job, and I'm grateful. But this isn't only *your* campaign, Serena. At the end of the day, it's mine. You're here to follow my directions. I love your enthusiasm—' *he'd said that before* '—but you go only as far as I deem reasonable. That's the only way this will work.'

His words, their love, her future, all pressed in. 'You decide what's best? I don't get a say?'

He shrugged. 'That's a little harsh. But, yes, that's the way it has to be.'

Overseas. Opportunity. Prove yourself. Believe.

The world became deathly quiet but for the ringing in her ears. She opened her mouth and the words spilled out.

'Then maybe we should call it a day.'

David held that breath.

Call it a day? What the hell was that supposed to mean? She was tired? Wanted to go home?

She'd decided to leave him?

That last thought was so absurd, he wanted to laugh. 'What are you talking about, call it a day?'

'I'll tell you…when you let go of my arms.'

He glanced down. His fingers dug into her flesh. Exercising the muscles strained at the back of his neck, he stepped away.

She chewed her lip, avoiding his eyes. 'I know you're happy with my performance here.'

'I've shown you every way I know how.'

Her gaze shot up. '*Please*. I need to get this out.'

He'd really upset her. He'd seen her naïve, saucy and spirited sides before. Looked as if now he was in for 'righteous indignation'.

It wasn't terminal. She could talk about this auction world charities idea. He'd listen, then placate her. Take her out to dinner. Show her how much he loved her. *Tell* her how much. He'd wanted to these past weeks. No excuse other than a stupid reluctance to leave himself open—vulnerable.

But more and more it became clear. The past was past.

Now was what mattered. Serena needed to hear those words as much as he needed to say them. She had his heart, fully and irrevocably. This relationship wasn't an affair but a prelude to their future.

'I've learned so much, grown so much since you gave me this opportunity…'

She talked on and he listened, even as he wondered how she'd look in a flowing white gown, ashen hair tressed up, big eyes brimming with happiness.

'Never in my wildest dreams,' she said, 'did I believe I was capable of so much, so soon. A big part was you and Jezz guiding and encouraging me, and I'm so grateful for that. But lately…' she winced '…I feel as though you're holding me back.'

What?

Ridiculous. She had it all wrong. Reassurance and T.L.C.—that was what she needed.

'My decisions regarding the campaign aren't about restraining you, Serena. They're about balancing maturity and experience with talent and drive. You've had some successes. That can do wonderful things for anyone's self-esteem. But sometimes…' he cushioned it with a gentle tone '…sometimes it can interfere with objectivity.'

Eyes glistening, she raised her chin. 'So, I'm full of myself now. I've lost all insight?'

He groaned under his breath. She was twisting things. That was not what he'd said. 'You need to listen to me—'

'No, *you* need to listen to *me*.' Colour stained her cheeks. Her breathing was shaky, as were her hands. He hated seeing her upset.

He stepped forward, but she stepped back.

'We each had our issues when we began this relationship,' she said. 'You knew I had a dream of working overseas. I accidentally let it slip when you gave me the job…I know you heard.'

Her travel plans? Yes, they'd worried him at first, but, 'We can work that out.'

'*How?* I need to prove myself, not to you, but for *me*. Part of that is doing what I always planned. You'll achieve *your* goal—the gold award, success for your company. You'll have your pride.' She slanted her head. 'What about my dream? Are my hopes less important?'

His blood turned cold. My God… 'You're serious. You're thinking about *leaving*? Just like that, out of the blue. Because I vetoed an idea?' It was crazy!

Her eyes pleaded with his. 'Not one idea. It's more than that. I feel as if you're not taking me seriously anymore. As if I'm turning into a prop or chattel. That's exactly what I *don't* want.'

Everything had been going so well. He'd fallen in love, opened his heart, and now she was threatening to leave?

He set his jaw. 'What do you want, Serena? Tell me. I'll fix it.'

She looked as if she hadn't understood.

'You don't get it. It *can't* be fixed. You've put your everything into your work, into *here*. I've put my heart into my goals, too, and they're going to take me someplace else. We're the same type of person. We want the same thing, just in separate ways that can't ever meet.'

I love you, damn it!

The words burned his tongue. He choked them down. He needed to sort this out without bringing sentiment into the mix. That would only help her argument.

She was so serious, so pale. Exhausted?

That must be it. Overworked and overwrought. He should have been firmer in making her have time off.

'You're not feeling well.' He coaxed her towards the door. 'We'll relax, have a quiet day. Take tomorrow. Take the week. Jezz can step in. I'll organize it.'

But she dug in her heels. 'Why is it that your pride is so important, but my ideals are lumps of clay, waiting to be shaped into someone else's mould?'

This argument wasn't reasonable. 'I never said that. I don't think that way.'

'Then why are you refusing to accept what I say? Why are you patronizing me? I'm not unwell. It's not this one idea. It's about what we each want. And they're different.'

He took a breath. All right. She needed to take it further. So, he'd sort it out from here.

A hand shovelled through his hair. 'Let's put everything on the table then. What do you want to do?'

Her eyes grew round and glassy. 'I've been offered a job.'

David's concentration warped, then a white-hot surge consumed his body as his heartbeat exploded. His hands shook. Clenching them, he premeditated a target. 'Jonathon Sturts.'

Serena pegged him square on. 'He spoke with Jezz a couple of days ago about a position for me in London. A responsible position without supervision.'

'Sturts went behind my *back*? When I get my hands around his throat—' David growled at the ceiling.

Her fingertips found his shirtfront. The contact immediately soothed him. His gaze meshed with hers. Did this mean she wouldn't take the job? Was this some game to give her an edge? She really didn't play fair.

His hand covered hers. 'We can work this out.'

'How? You move to London too? I don't know how long I'll stay or where it will lead me. Are you going to leave your life here behind to follow me?'

'That's obviously not the answer.'

'Because it doesn't suit you? Maybe I should decline Jonathon's offer, stay here and we could both grow to resent that decision and each other. We wouldn't be happy. Then again, you might get bored after a few more months—'

When he dragged her to him, his arms around her had never felt more right. Her body—so supple and tempting, pressed close to his—told him, despite her words, that she wanted him too. Would always want him. And he would always want her.

He challenged her. 'You want to leave me?'

Tears rimmed her eyes. 'I don't want to. I don't feel I have a choice.'

The knife twisted in his gut. 'You could *do* that? Just walk out?' She wasn't talking sense.

She groaned as his mouth trailed her cheek. 'It's not that simple.' She wreathed away, or was it against him when he nipped her jaw? 'I told you it wouldn't be.'

'You wouldn't regret leaving me behind?' He kissed her deeply as his hand scooped down over the curve below her tailbone.

She broke the kiss. 'Don't do this. It won't change my mind.'

Keep her here. Make her see.

'Then say goodbye to me properly, Serena. If you can walk out, I deserve at least that.'

He coaxed her, found her lips again, and she began to move. When she came up for air, he hid a smile. He *would* convince her.

He didn't share.

'You wouldn't respect me.' She hummed in her throat as he kissed her again, then murmured, 'I wouldn't respect myself.'

He let her see his understanding smile. 'We'll talk about that later.'

Hurt sparked in her eyes. She pushed against him hard and strode away.

'*Serena.*' He reached out a hand. 'Come back. Serena, we're not finished!'

The door slammed closed behind her. By the time he yanked it open, his heart was pounding and she was gone.

CHAPTER SIXTEEN

SERENA'S father looked bone-weary when he opened his front door. His furrowed brow and salt-and-pepper hair, all askew, told her he must have fallen asleep sitting up in his rocker. He seemed so old, almost a different man. Then he smiled, and it was her dad again, just the way she remembered.

He held out his arms. 'Serena, what are you doing here on a week night?'

'I need to talk to you.' They hugged. 'Can I come in?'

He patted her back, then drew away. 'Well, this *is* a surprise.' She stepped inside and he led the way through into the house she knew so well. 'I wasn't expecting to see you till Christmas.' His tone lowered. 'Nothing wrong, I hope.'

She withered inside. 'Not exactly.'

'Has something unravelled between you and Carly again? Last time you two had a tiff you were lost for days.' His voice took on that 'father-knows-best' tone. 'I say call her up and sort it out. Time's too short and pride doesn't help.'

'Carly and I haven't had an argument in ten years.' She trailed a finger over the oak sideboard in the hall as they passed. 'It's my job.'

The lines branching from his eyes deepened. 'But it

was going so well when you visited on my birthday. Did they sack you?'

Before she had time to answer, he poopooed it with a hand and moved towards his favourite chair. Serena couldn't remember a time when it hadn't graced the same spot in the middle of this modestly sized living room.

'If that's the way they feel,' he said, 'good riddance.' After resettling a stamp album from the rocker's arm to the floor, he lowered himself down and clicked a switch. The footrest popped and his brown vinyl slippers flew up. 'We'll work on your résumé. You've got lots of talent and determination. We just need to point it in the right direction.'

She forced the words over the stone lodged in her throat. 'I resigned.'

About to collect his tea, his hand froze. He turned and drilled her with a look. 'Do you think that's wise? Good jobs are so difficult to come by. If you'd talked to me first, we could have looked at all the pros and cons. Worked out a plan. Every decision we make in our lives affects the choices we have in the future.'

She fell back into the couch. Alpine clock on the wall, pineapple doilies on the TV, a comforting smell of yesterday that hadn't faded. Thank God she had home.

'I know about choices and the future, Dad. That's why I had to leave. I was offered a dream job in London.'

He frowned. 'Three months ago this was your dream job.' He sipped his tea, then held high his cup. 'Want one?'

She shook her head. 'I've moved on since then.' So quickly, now she could barely think straight. 'This new position is senior. Great money, plus so many of the wonderful places I want to see will be close enough to visit.'

Brace yourself for his levelling words of wisdom. He'd

say how he thought she might have done the wrong thing. That she could have acted hastily. But she'd made up her mind. Nothing in this world would stop her.

Evaluating her over his cup, he downed the rest of his tea, then smacked his lips. 'Well, now, that sounds wonderful.'

She almost collapsed onto the floor. Really? He seemed so sure. 'You honestly think so?'

'Certainly.' His cup clattered into its saucer on the cedar side-table.

He wasn't going to shoot her plan down? Not even bring up her bouts of homesickness? Surely they'd come to mind. Since making her snap decision, she'd certainly found lots of reasons to stay. Leaving her home, her dad, Carly, Jezz, her job, that special client and the campaign. But one reason shone out from the rest like a blinding beacon.

David.

To know he would never hold her, they would never kiss or talk or tease or make love again, was too depressing to consider. He was so special. Hell, he was perfect. If only he'd come along years from now when she'd got all this out of her system.

From the portrait above the buffet, Marion Stevens gazed down with that soft smile and kind green eyes. Serena sighed. Would her mother be pleased with her decision?

She clasped her hands and set them in her lap.

What was done was done. She'd annihilated her relationship with David in a five-minute flash. What she'd seen as his lack of faith, he'd viewed as a necessary wing-clipping. Had she overreacted? Had her successes led to a sense of overworth?

Still, her drive to go harder and reach higher had won

her that position in the first place. Those were the qualities Jonathon wanted working for his company, too.

She puffed out a breath. Whatever the answer, she'd made her choice—given the circumstances surrounding yesterday's showdown, the only choice she could.

Her dad crossed his ankles. 'When do you leave?'

She pigeon-toed her feet and tapped her toes. 'Soon as possible. My passport's up-to-date and my new boss is looking after any other documents.'

He nodded. 'It's what you've been working toward all these years. I remember you talking to Mum about it.'

Though she knew the pendant was still at David's house, she reached for her gold heart. When she'd rung last night, he'd told her not to bother coming back to work to finish up. Jezz had been on the phone by nine this morning. Serena's belongings from the office had been delivered to her apartment by ten. The heart would be a reason to see David one last time.

But *would* he see her?

Just as she was stubborn, David was a man built on personal strength and pride. After his efforts to convince her yesterday, he wouldn't fall down on his knees and beg. He'd take her decision and seal off his heart. He would dispose of her love, get on with his life, which was what she wanted. Right?

Her father threaded his hands over the sash of his blue chequered gown. 'That job working part-time at the chicken place, all those assignments and all-night study sessions before exams. You did it harder than most, but you succeeded, and will go on succeeding. I'm so proud of you, Renie.'

Her throat constricted as tears stung her eyes. Those last

few words touched her as nothing else could. He'd said them before, the night she'd won the award for the essay, when they'd sat side by side, squeezing each other's hands at the funeral, and at other times, too. She knew now he meant it with all his heart. And it helped. Still…

'You haven't got even one word of warning, or a single concern that I'm doing the wrong thing. London's a long way away.' Her stomach twinged thinking about it.

'Thirteen thousand miles, I believe. But only a phone call away.'

Serena gazed at the floor. 'Phones aren't nearly as reassuring as knowing someone's available in the flesh.'

Such a big step and it had all happened so fast. What if she hated her new job? What if she failed? She'd come so far—would she *ever* lose those kinds of doubts?

'It's a big decision, but it can only be yours.' A wan smile eased across his face. 'Doesn't mean I won't worry.'

Eyes on hers, he lifted and sipped from his empty cup. He frowned and put it back down.

He was tired. She ought to go. 'I'll see you again before I leave, give you contact numbers and an address.'

He rocked out of his chair to see her to the door. When they reached the adjoining corridor, he turned the wrong way.

Serena laughed. 'Aren't you going to see me out before you go to bed?'

His smile was watery. 'Sorry, sweetheart. I've had a big week. Lectures and papers to mark.'

'You are almost sixty. You should retire from teaching and take it easy.' He'd been fifteen years older than her mother. Despite the age difference, despite everything, they'd been so happy.

They hugged at the door, a big bear hug as they'd shared

when she was his little girl what seemed like a lifetime ago and yet only yesterday.

He waved goodbye as she moved towards her car. 'Be careful.'

She called over her shoulder and waved. 'I will.'

'And don't be out all night. I worry when you're not home by twelve.'

Cool fingers tripped up her spine. All the little mistakes and absent-mindedness suddenly added up. She stopped mid-step and swung around. Her father was closing the door.

'Dad?' Heart in her throat, she started back, forcing herself not to run.

He blinked over at her. 'Did you forget something, sweetheart?'

She studied the man who'd done his best to guide and protect her after his wife had passed away. And before that, the horse-riding lessons, the endless help with homework, the bedtime stories of how he would get homesick, too, if ever he had to go away.

Smoothing the hair at his temple, she willed back the tears and smiled. 'Sometimes I do forget, but I remember now. Let's go back inside.'

CHAPTER SEVENTEEN

'HELLO, David. Hope I'm not interrupting.'

Serena's kept her chin high and pain hidden as David glanced over. Out on his terrace, sitting at an eight-seater setting, he was making paper planes. His jeans were worn, his T-shirt white and looking finer than any Italian suit she'd ever seen him in. Masculine, virile, he appeared almost dangerous.

When his gaze met hers, a smile lifted one corner of his mouth. But his bare feet, crossed at the ankles, remained raised on the chair opposite. The smile didn't reach his eyes.

He weighed the plane in his hand as she approached. 'Serena. What's it been? Three weeks?'

'Four.' To the day. A month since their argument and her decision to leave. A month of little food or sleep or peace.

He eyed her up and down, then continued inspecting the line of his plane. 'Can I have Gil bring you a drink? Coffee, tea?'

The back of her throat closed, but she didn't flinch at his insult. Not so long ago he'd made certain to offer her exactly what she liked. She wouldn't jog his memory. He didn't want to be reminded.

'I'm fine, thank you.'

The plane left his hand and sailed over the scarlet bougainvillea out of sight. Concentrating on its flight, elbows on armrests, David clasped his hands near his chin and nodded as if he'd accomplished something grand. His gaze snapped back and he indicated that she should sit.

The noonday sun warmed her arms and face as she neared the table and glanced around. 'Where's Sylvie?'

David set aside the extra sheets of paper. 'Guess she doesn't like goodbyes.' As the stab in her stomach eased she took a seat. 'So, did you hear about the awards last night?'

'This morning's business editorial featured a spread.' Half proud, half strangely disconnected, she'd read and reread it for over an hour. 'You took home the gold,' she said as he reached for a nearby handset. 'Congratulations.'

'Gil, have you got that coffee? Extra strong and hot. Thanks.' He replaced the receiver. 'Gold…yes. Thanks largely to your efforts. You did a brilliant job with that campaign.'

His words were neither goading nor heartfelt, rather almost wooden. Was he enjoying using this tactic to make her uncomfortable? What had she expected? Harsh words? Raised voices? Colourful flowers along with his card?

Tonight?

She swallowed. 'I appreciate you saying that.' *And that you got what you wanted.*

Gilbert, wearing an unfamiliar dark shirt, appeared with a huge mug on a tray. 'Anything else, sir?'

'No, nothing.' As the mug lowered David snapped his fingers. 'Oh, can you make sure that jacket and trousers I ordered last week are ready?' He caught the time on his watch. 'That luncheon's in an hour.'

Gilbert's eyebrows jumped. 'I'll organize it.' He redirected his attention. 'May I get you anything, Serena?'

Rather than ushering, Gilbert had walked by her side when he'd escorted her out onto the terrace, perhaps his way of saying, without getting involved, that he liked her and cared.

'Thanks, Gilbert.' Her chair scraped back and she found her feet. 'I should just collect my things and—'

'No rush.' Thigh muscles in soft denim flexed as David uncrossed his ankles and sat up. 'It's only a small victory get-together. I think I partied a little too hard last night as it is.' The thumb and index finger rubbing his brow dropped to collect the mug.

Yes, there were smudges beneath his eyes. Why let a break-up get in the way of a good time, right?

He blew at the steam. 'Did you get my bonus?' He sipped and swallowed. 'I wanted to express my gratitude for all you'd done.'

Over the top of that big black mug he looked at her—so calm, so okay with it all. His bonus? She'd received it. A phone call, a few key strokes, and the funds had been returned. Now she no longer worked for him, she didn't want his money, not for any reason, particularly the one he was suggesting. Sleeping with David had been a joy, not a service.

Play it cool.

Moving towards the railing, she deflected the focus away from herself. 'Your clients must be pleased.'

'Still are. You're in touch with Jezz, yes?'

No need to answer; he knew they were friends.

She turned and rested her elbows on the railing at her back as he unfolded from his chair.

He slipped his hands into his rear pockets. 'She's doing

an incredible job, thank God.' Serena's senses began buzzing as he moved towards her. 'Don't know what I would have done without her. Of course, I understand you had your reasons for leaving.' His smile was tight. 'People always do.'

Did she deserve this? He was comparing her to Olivia What's-her-name and that wasn't fair. She hadn't flippantly tossed it in like that other woman. He'd been hurt before. Well, so had she. So where did the blame for this impasse really lie? With her?

How many women would leap at the chance to drop everything to pursue a relationship with someone like him? But then how many men like David would drop their lives to follow a woman with equal drive and passion?

Her heart bled, but no matter how she tried, no matter how much anyone might think she ought to get over herself and gamble on a life of luxury with a rich man, she simply couldn't.

Could an artist say they'd happily not paint again, or a writer never tell another story when the person they'd sacrificed for was still fulfilling *their* dreams? It couldn't work.

Maybe she didn't love David enough? But, if that were true, maybe he didn't love her enough either?

Stomach in knots, she found her voice. 'It's wonderful that everything's worked out for your agency.' Despite everything, she would always wish him well. 'After a decade of hard work, you deserve it.'

Forearms resting on the railing ledge, he leant forward, laced his hands and squinted at the stark blue sky. 'What about you?' A pulse jumped in his cheek. 'You must be gearing up to head off overseas?'

She eased out a sigh. Pretending that her plans weren't

delayed was a waste of time—he'd find out anyway. She'd rather not be a coward and tell him now.

'I'm not taking the London job.'

David's head kicked back as if someone punched his nose. His arms left the ledge and he drew up tall. 'Did you get a better offer?'

He grinned, but his eyes were dark. Was that his heart she saw thumping beneath the white interlock?

'My father's ill,' she told him. 'I've taken him for tests.'

Brow knitting, his gaze flickered over her. 'Did they find out what's wrong?'

She nodded. 'A growth needs to be removed.'

When his hands enfolded hers, she hated herself but gave in to his comfort, and her pressure valve, which had been cranked up to overload, eased off to 'almost coping'.

His voice was deep and filled with genuine concern. 'What's the prognosis?'

'The surgeon can't give guarantees, but it's not aggressive. Because of its size and location, he's hopeful Dad will make a full recovery.'

His thumbs stroked the tops of her clenched hands as his lowered voice cascaded through her. Oh, God, it felt so good, so right.

'Is there anything I can do?'

She set her teeth. 'Nothing.' Her hands slid away. 'Other than being forgetful, Dad seems fine. The operation is scheduled a month from now. His blood pressure needs to come way down.'

He studied her. 'You're staying in Sydney?'

'For now. I told Jonathon about my situation—that, unfortunately, the timing's not right.'

'Meaning?'

He knew damn well what she meant. 'Meaning if—' she corrected herself '—*when* Dad's well again, I'll get back on track.'

'To London.'

Her hands clenched. 'To *somewhere*.'

Grabbing a coffee on 42nd Street on her way to work. Visiting the Louvre in Paris, a twenty-minute stroll from her apartment. Running through puddles in the afternoon rain to catch a London bus. Those visions had kept her going, kept her strong, kept her focused.

Don't you understand? I have to do this.

His gaze roamed her face. Finally he nodded. 'Need a job in the meantime?'

And risk being close to you?

'Jonathon's offered me a position at Mixem's.'

A vein at David's temple pulsed. Was he about to thump around like a caveman?

Finally shunting a hand through his hair, he let out a breath. 'Just promise me you won't listen to any tracks with him in booth D.'

His smile was lopsided, but the storm in his eyes said he was deadly serious—*his* territory, *his* experience, *his* girl.

'Jonathon's fine.' He wouldn't make a pass. 'I think a man knows if he has a chance with a woman.'

David's expression deepened and she read the message in his eyes. *Do I have chance?*

Mounting tension finally sparked alight and flared. An air of awareness seemed to settle over them as the questions echoed through her mind.

Does he have a chance? Is it over? Is this the last time we'll see each other?

As his intensity reached out she leant forward, drawn

by his strength, compelled by instinct and heartache so raw, she felt completely empty.

His gaze lowered to trail her mouth, telling her that with a word or a whimper he would crush her in and prove what they'd experienced before was an entrée compared to the banquet he'd share with her now.

A word, some sign, and their affair would begin again.

Would begin...and would end. Nothing had changed. Maybe not this week or next month, but she *would* go and he would stay. No use hoping he'd wait for her. His pride would be so badly burned, he'd never trust her again. She knew him well enough to be certain of that.

A cramp wrenched deep inside and she had to look away.

God, oh, God, do I really want to give him up? Can I give him up?

David's crooked finger raised her chin. His brow was smooth, his smile resigned. He'd never looked more handsome. 'You're right. A man *does* know when he has chance.'

The energy drained from her body as he left her to cross the terrace and pick up the handset.

'Gilbert, Serena's ready to leave. Have you got her belongings together?' A pause. 'I'll send her on her way.'

With a mountain weighing on her back, she moved to join him. She waited for him to—

What? Shake her hand? Wish her *bon voyage*?

Nothing more needed to be said.

She swallowed back stinging tears and turned towards the doors.

'Serena...wait.'

Her step faltered as cool air rushed into her lungs. Pulse tripping over itself, she spun back around.

Will he say it?

He stood before her, a tower, a refuge, the man she loved. But what was the message in his eyes?

She blinked before her gaze dropped to the pool of gold nestled in his outstretched palm.

'I know how much this means to you,' he said. 'I kept it aside so it wouldn't be misplaced.' The pendant fell into her hand. 'Here's your heart back.'

CHAPTER EIGHTEEN

'BOARDING pass, please.'

Serena set her hand luggage down, fished around at the top of her handbag and offered over the pass.

The statuesque stewardess attending the departure gate at Sydney International checked it, smiled, then handed the pass back. 'Enjoy your flight.'

Well, she'd try her best.

Moving down the enclosed jetway, Serena double checked that the air-sickness pills Jezz had recommended were in the front zipper of her bag. The caution read: 'May cause drowsiness.' An enforced sleep could only do her good.

As she re-zipped the compartment her glasses fell off her bowed head to bounce on the carpet at her feet. She swooped on the frames, but another hand beat her to them.

Eyes locked, they straightened at the same time.

The middle-aged man pushed his own frames higher upon his nose. 'Hey, you don't want anyone standing on those.' He placed them in her hand. 'Glasses can be a pain in the caboose—keeping them clean, wondering where you've left them. But if you're anything like me, you're bat-blind without them.'

He fell in step beside her.

'I usually wear contacts.' But she'd run out of disposables last week and hadn't bothered getting more. Lately, it was an effort to brush her hair. 'I haven't worn these in years. Guess the arms are loose. Probably need a new pair.'

Before she presented the pass to the flight attendant at the doorway, Serena turned to the man and touched the glasses perched on her nose. 'Thanks for your trouble.'

Halfway down the first aisle, she found her seat. Hand luggage locked away—now she could slip on some flight slippers and retreat into her own shell.

The man appeared again. 'Hey, looks like we'll be flight buddies.' He showed her his pass. They looked at hers. Yep, seats side by side. 'Don't suppose you'd give up the window?' He was short, well-dressed, with a nasally voice and the smell of tea-tree oil.

'I'd rather not.' She sidled into her seat. 'This is my first flight.'

He shuffled in beside her. 'Excellent!' He dropped a lozenge on his tongue. 'Throat infection.'

Serena peered out the window.

'Hey, so this must be your first trip to Paris?'

Serena's teeth caught the inside of her lips and she nodded.

'Staying long?' he persisted.

'Only a week.'

'What?' She turned to see his jowls working as he sucked. 'That's not *nearly* long enough. I remember my first trip over.' He rubbed his paunch and chuckled. 'Met this lady, stunner she was. Took me to the Moulin Rouge and told me she could dance—'

'My father's going in for an operation.' It just came out. Call her precious, but she couldn't bear to hear about anyone else's love life, didn't want to know about someone else's happiness, when she felt so lost.

'Operation, huh?' *Suck, suck.* 'Nothing serious, I hope.'

'We're hopeful it will be a success. But he needs to re-cuperate. Maybe go back a second time.'

She gazed out at the grey tarmac absorbing the sunshine and rested her forehead against the window. Homesick already. Homesick for David. She missed him so much.

'Man, that's tough.' Out of the corner of her eye, she saw the man pop another cough drop. 'Sounds like you're the one looking after him.' She nodded at the empty luggage train winding back towards the terminal. 'So you decided to refuel your engines before settling down to the job?'

Not a job. Her dad had been there for her. Now she'd be there for him. She was only pleased she could be.

'I didn't book my flight. My father insisted I have this week away.' He might drive her nuts with his warnings, but she'd come to understand that his advice was part of his love and thoughtfulness. She was lucky to have had him growing up. *And*, he would be there in her bright future.

No more doubt monsters. Her father would be fine. She'd have a fabulous time in France, visit the Louvre, stand in the shadow of the Eiffel Tower, get on with her life, and soon she'd forget all about…

Her eyes drifted closed as her forehead rolled back and forth against the glass.

Forget…please, forget.

An eternity later, the jet was at cruising altitude. A blanket lay over her lap, a barely read magazine on top of that. Three sickness pills and she needed to take off the glasses to rub her gritty eyes.

In the seat alongside, her new friend removed his earphones and pushed up out of his seat. 'I'm off to stretch my legs. Can I bring you back a drink? You don't want to get dehydrated.'

Her father had told her the same thing. She smiled. 'A water. Thanks.'

A scattering of clouds lay below. The sky was a dome of blemish-free blue that knew no limits. Just like her life. But had she given up too much to achieve her goals?

Could dreams change?

Even a little?

She slid her lenses up and down her silk sleeve and thought of the woman she'd come to love and respect. Jezz was *still* achieving and had no regrets about not marrying, but she had been careful choosing her parting words at the terminal earlier. 'Some people say you can't have everything. Don't believe them.'

Everything…

Proving herself had been everything. Pride was everything to David. It had cost them what they deserved to pursue. And she couldn't think of any way around it. Perhaps sadder still, neither had he.

Immersed in memories, Serena jumped when something cool—her drink—pressed against her hand. She accepted it, mumbled a thank you, then blinked and frowned.

A flute? Filled with…was it—

'Wine and red soda?'

Her heartbeat froze, then belted against her ribs. She swung around and a battery of fireworks exploded through her body. She felt faint and born again at the same incredible time.

'*David?*' She breathed his name as she slotted her glasses back on, just to make sure.

'Glasses, huh? *Very* sexy.' His eyes smiled across at her as he indicated the seat. 'May I?'

Her voice had vanished so she simply nodded. A dream. It had to be. The pills had knocked her out—that was the only explanation. This *couldn't* be real.

When he was seated, she touched his forearm, hot and solid below the cuff of a rolled chambray sleeve. Olive skin, dark hair, hot scent that reminded her of his chest and his kiss. David was *really* sitting beside her.

She forced the cogs of her seized brain forward. 'What are you doing here?'

He adjusted his seat and got comfortable. 'Flying to Paris.'

Mildly hysterical, she pressed the butt of her hand to her temple and shook her head. 'I don't understand.'

'Then let me explain.'

Cupping her cheeks, he drew her near. After those long lonely weeks, his mouth claiming hers felt better than heaven. More beautiful than a song. Giving in to the wonder, she savoured his caress along with every delicious promise it seemed to hold.

The hot pad of one finger ran around her jaw as he so slowly broke the kiss. His soft, sultry smile was hypnotic. 'Getting the picture now?'

'I'm not sure.' Warmed to her core, she sighed out a smile. 'Maybe more explaining...'

His expression was more earnest than bad boy when he lifted her hand and brushed his lips over the palm. 'When I got that award, I thought I'd feel better. I'd survived tough times before. I could get over this. Over you. But as the days passed I realized I was making the biggest mistake of my life, letting my stupid pride get in the way of the two most important things in my life.' She shivered when he tipped forward and murmured against her ear, 'You, and you.'

His nose curved around the shell as he drew away.

She shook herself out of happy-land enough to ask, 'So, you decided to surprise me on an a plane?'

One brow arched. 'Thought you'd think it was romantic.'

'And stay in Paris with me for a week?'

'I'm making *us* our number one priority. We can't get away from each other here. We can, and will, work this out.'

Reality came crashing down. She pulled back. 'How, David? We've been through this.' *Serena, for God's sake, just shut up!* But she couldn't. They couldn't back away from it. 'I still want to work overseas.'

'Then I'll keep myself busy overseas too, as long as you come home to me every night.' His hand found hers and squeezed. 'You were right. I can buy another business. An air carrier or small airline some place. I don't have to prove myself to the advertising industry. That was the excuse I used to drive myself. You're what matters to me. You're my dream. Let me in, Serena. Let me love you.'

Her nose prickled with a rush of coming tears. She gulped down a laugh. 'You'd do that for *me*?'

'Only every day of my life.' His fingers fanned around her cheek while his gaze dropped from her hair to her eyes. 'I am so sorry. I should have made myself clear and said it before, should have done something about it sooner. I love you. I fought against it. With my hang-ups and your passion I knew we'd be in for a rough as well as wonderful time.'

A drop escaped the corner of her eye. Her words were more a wonder-filled breath. 'You love me?'

'From your dimples right down to your toes.' His grin hooked at one side. 'Especially your toes. And I love the way you manage to look both efficient and as sexy as hell when you head a meeting. The way you won't back down when you think that you're right. I love the way you make me feel…incredibly light, incredibly right.'

When he reached over and kissed her again, she dissolved, completely, irreversibly. She was exactly where she wanted to be—nothing left to prove and everything to live for.

Their embrace eased into kisses dotted on the side of her mouth, her cheek, her chin. 'Serena?'

Did she have to wake up?

Eyes closed, she urged him closer. 'Hmm?'

'Is there anything you'd like to share with me? Something you'd like to say?'

Her eyes drifted open. 'Like, where's a shower?'

He chuckled as he nuzzled into her hair. 'You bet, with lots of soap. But, right now I was thinking more along the lines of…'

Her fingers touched his lips. 'I love you, too. Love you with everything in my heart.' Memories of her days without him vanished like some magical mist. All that mattered was that they were together and he was about to kiss her again.

'Hey, buddy, that's my seat.'

They looked across to find her new friend standing in the aisle and holding her water.

David turned in his seat. 'It's an inconvenience, I know. But if you can be patient, maybe take another seat, I'm about to propose to my girl.'

Serena gasped. *'Propose?'*

He took her glass, passed it to the man without taking his eyes from hers, then clasped both her hands to his chest. 'Serena, will you marry me?'

Every doubt she'd ever known vanished when she replied. 'When?'

His face eased into one of his bone-melting smiles. 'We'll shop in Paris for the perfect ring.'

'Hey, that's all very nice,' the man said, 'but I paid for that seat.'

David's big shoulders rotated again. 'Why don't you go upstairs and tell the stewardess that David Miles made a mistake and his seat is now yours?'

The man raised his brows, sipped the drink and grinned. 'They have nice platters in first class.'

When David focused on her again, Serena's mind still whirled and her throat was clogged with emotion. 'You'd give up your life here for me? You'd sit in economy?'

'I'd sit any damn place you want. Do anything you want.' A wicked glint sparked in his eyes. 'Which gives me an idea.'

She grinned and nibbled his lower lip. 'Are you thinking what I think you're thinking? I'm not registered with the Mile High Club.'

His arms curved around her waist. 'That won't be a problem. New members join free. No forms. No delay.' His smile grazed her lips as he removed her glasses, then pulled the blanket over their heads. 'Houston, we have lift-off.'

I ♥ HARLEQUIN *Presents*

BROUGHT TO YOU BY FANS OF
HARLEQUIN PRESENTS.

We are its editors and authors
and biggest fans—and we'd
love to hear from YOU!

**Subscribe today to our online blog at
www.iheartpresents.com**

REQUEST YOUR FREE BOOKS!

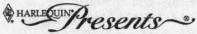 

2 FREE NOVELS PLUS 2 FREE GIFTS!

YES! Please send me 2 FREE Harlequin Presents® novels and my 2 FREE gifts (gifts are worth about $10). After receiving them, if I don't wish to receive any more books, I can return the shipping statement marked "cancel". If I don't cancel, I will receive 6 brand-new novels every month and be billed just $4.05 per book in the U.S. or $4.74 per book in Canada, plus 25¢ shipping and handling per book and applicable taxes, if any*. That's a savings of close to 15% off the cover price! I understand that accepting the 2 free books and gifts places me under no obligation to buy anything. I can always return a shipment and cancel at any time. Even if I never buy another book, the two free books and gifts are mine to keep forever.   106 HDN ERRW   306 HDN ERRL

Name	(PLEASE PRINT)	
Address		Apt. #
City	State/Prov.	Zip/Postal Code

Signature (if under 18, a parent or guardian must sign)

Mail to the Harlequin Reader Service:
IN U.S.A.: P.O. Box 1867, Buffalo, NY 14240-1867
IN CANADA: P.O. Box 609, Fort Erie, Ontario L2A 5X3

Not valid to current subscribers of Harlequin Presents books.

Want to try two free books from another line?
Call 1-800-873-8635 or visit www.morefreebooks.com.

* Terms and prices subject to change without notice. N.Y. residents add applicable sales tax. Canadian residents will be charged applicable provincial taxes and GST. This offer is limited to one order per household. All orders subject to approval. Credit or debit balances in a customer's account(s) may be offset by any other outstanding balance owed by or to the customer. Please allow 4 to 6 weeks for delivery. Offer available while quantities last.

Your Privacy: Harlequin Books is committed to protecting your privacy. Our Privacy Policy is available online at www.eHarlequin.com or upon request from the Reader Service. From time to time we make our lists of customers available to reputable third parties who may have a product or service of interest to you. If you would prefer we not share your name and address, please check here. ☐

HP08

HARLEQUIN *Presents*

He's successful, powerful—and extremely sexy....
He also happens to be her boss! Used to getting his
own way, he'll demand what he wants from her—
in the boardroom and the bedroom....

Watch the sparks fly as these couples
work together—and play together!

IN BED WITH
THE BOSS

Don't miss any of the stories in April's collection!

MISTRESS IN PRIVATE
by JULIE COHEN

IN BED WITH HER ITALIAN BOSS
by KATE HARDY

MY TALL DARK GREEK BOSS
by ANNA CLEARY

HOUSEKEEPER TO
THE MILLIONAIRE
by LUCY MONROE

Available April 8
wherever books are sold.